A Way between Worlds

Also by Melanie Crowder

The Lighthouse between the Worlds
Three Pennies
A Nearer Moon
Parched
Audacity
An Uninterrupted View of the Sky

A Way between Worlds

Melanie Crowder

Atheneum Books for Young Readers

New York London Toronto Sydney New Delhi

A
atheneum ATHENEUM BOOKS FOR YOUNG READERS
An imprint of Simon & Schuster Children's Publishing Division
1230 Avenue of the Americas, New York, New York 10020

ATHENEUM BOOKS FOR YOUNG READERS
is a registered trademark of Simon & Schuster, Inc. Atheneum logo
is a trademark of Simon & Schuster, Inc.
For information about special discounts for bulk purchases, please contact
Simon & Schuster Special Sales at 1-866-506-1949
or business@simonandschuster.com.
The Simon & Schuster Speakers Bureau can bring authors to your
live event. For more information or to book an event, contact
the Simon & Schuster Speakers Bureau at 1-866-248-3049 or
visit our website at www.simonspeakers.com.
Book design by Debra Sfetsios-Conover
The text for this book was set in Palatino LT.
The illustrations for this book were digitally rendered.
Manufactured in the United States of America
0819 FFG
First Edition
2 4 6 8 10 9 7 5 3 1
Library of Congress Cataloging-in-Publication Data
Names: Crowder, Melanie, author.
Title: A way between worlds / Melanie Crowder.
Description: First edition. | New York : Atheneum Books for Young
Readers, [2019] | Series: Lighthouse Keepers | Summary: Griffin and Fi
must navigate magical worlds of mist, water, vines, and fire, seeking their
own gifts as they try to save themselves and every single world.
Identifiers: LCCN 2018061502 | ISBN 9781534405189 (hardcover) |
ISBN 9781534405202 (eBook)
Subjects: | CYAC: Adventure and adventurers—Fiction. | Magic—Fiction. |
Fantasy. | Science fiction.
Classification: LCC PZ7.C885382 Way 2019 | DDC [Fic]—dc23
LC record available at https://lccn.loc.gov/2018061502

For Addie

GRIFFIN

I F GRIFFIN HAD learned anything about magic, it's that you can't trust it. Not one bit.

His eyes fluttered open after a too-short nap and the ceiling was *right there,* his nose smashed against it, and his toes, too. He floated on a plane of mist high above his bed, with nothing but air holding him up. Griffin jerked in panic, flinging his arms out to both sides, grabbing at anything in reach.

Laughter tittered below. He swung his head around, banging it against the ceiling. Three children scurried out the door, shrieking and giggling while Griffin watched helplessly from above. They wore gauzy layers of spun spider silk like everybody here, the loose edges trailing in the air as they whipped around the corner and out of sight.

Without any warning, Griffin dropped out of the air, the curled corners of his mom's drawings fluttering as he plopped onto the feather bed below. He scampered off the bed in case those little magic workers came back for a second try. (Not that he could do anything about it if they did.) But still, he felt better facing them on his feet.

He'd only been on this world for four days, and that was already four days too many. Griffin shivered. His body still hadn't adjusted to the chill of Caligo after the dry heat of Somni. But he'd put up with the cold (and the pesky kids) if it meant he and his mom were safe.

Griffin shuffled out the open doorway and to the edge of the floating island where they were staying, shading his eyes against the glare. A swarm of birds as tiny as bees spiraled like a tumbleweed, chasing a cluster of windblown seeds. The kids were long gone, seated in one of the shallow boats that rode the currents of air through the city in the sky. In the distance, the lighthouse tower rose out of a bank of crisp, white mist. The lens at the top swiveled, winking as it turned.

The lighthouse. That's what had started all this trouble. Well, not *that* one. The one back home on the Oregon coast that Griffin and his dad took care of.

He loved that lighthouse—it was cool in an old-timey sort of way, and it was all theirs, his and his dad's.

Of course, he'd always assumed it was an ordinary lighthouse. Why wouldn't it be? But then his dad was sucked through the glass, and Griffin found out that the lens was a portal between Earth and a bunch of other worlds, and that his parents, Philip and Katherine Fenn, were part of a secret society tasked with guarding the portal against invaders from those other worlds.

Griffin had gone after his dad, though he barely knew anything about Somni, the world Philip had been pulled into, or the wicked priests who'd kidnapped him. It had been like a nightmare, losing his dad after his mom had died only three years before. But if the priests hadn't kidnapped Philip, maybe Griffin never would have discovered that his mom wasn't really dead. Years before, Katherine had been kidnapped by the same priests, who'd planned to use her lifelong study of Fresnel lenses to unlock the portal's magic.

Griffin shuddered. That's the last thing anyone on any world needed—those priests getting ahold of more magic. It was bad enough that if you didn't have a way to protect your mind, the priests could control your every move and use that power to attack and colonize every world in their reach.

Griffin turned his back on the mists and peeked into the room beside his. Katherine was sprawled on the floor, books scattered around her as she soaked up all she could about the years she'd missed. Her dark hair was tucked behind her ears and she hummed absently while she read. Relief rushed through Griffin at the sight of her there, alive and getting well.

If only his dad was here. The family had just been reunited—they weren't supposed to be separated on different worlds again so soon. But the Somnite rebels needed Philip's help. He had to stay behind to make glass pendants that would shield their minds, protecting the people of Somni from falling back under the priests' spell. It had to be this way, at least for a little while longer. Still, Griffin wouldn't stop worrying until his whole family was together again and those wicked priests were gone for good.

Katherine glanced up. "You're awake!" she exclaimed, promptly shutting the book in her lap and setting it aside with the rest.

Griffin nodded. His mom had been so fragile when she first arrived—half starved and covered in bone-deep bruises. The mists had wrapped around her, healing her hurts and making her stronger each day. She was still terribly thin, and sometimes in the middle of a conversation, her face would blanch, her shoulders hunching over like a wounded animal. Her nightmares woke them both.

They were supposed to have gone home through the portal, to Earth, where Griffin could get her to a hospital. But the Levitator had other plans (not that he'd bothered to share what those were) and he'd pulled Griffin and Katherine through the portal to Caligo.

They were stuck here.

So each day Griffin and his mom took one of the little boats on a tour of the floating islands to see the strange birds in the mews, stroll through the markets, or visit the observatory, where the glare of the mists was blocked out and they could peer into the purple nebulae and red stars and blue planets spinning above. It wasn't like on Earth, where you had to wait for night to see the stars. On Caligo, they were always there, pinpricks piercing the black floating above the mist. If Griffin had been one of those kids obsessed with rockets and satellites and aliens, he would have spent all his time at the observatory, looking deeper into space than anyone on Earth could.

But the real reason they ventured out every day was to check in on Fi. Griffin had met the young spy on Somni while he was desperately searching for his dad. She'd been working for the Vinean resistance, disguised as one of the servants. He hadn't trusted her at first, but without Fi, none of the Fenns would have escaped.

It was hard for Griffin to be stuck on Caligo, but it was even worse for Fi. At that very moment, the resistance was fighting to save their home world of Vinea. And she was here, powerless to help them.

As if Katherine could read his mind, she brushed past Griffin, resting a hand against his cheek before stepping into a boat waiting at the island's edge. "Let's see if Fi wants to visit the library with us, hmmm? Leónie told me there's an entire section on the seven other worlds—one floor for each. Over the years, the Levitators have written down everything they observed through the portal. Imagine, Griffin— they've peered into Glacies, and Arida, and, *oh*—do you think even if they could see into Stella that they'd actually *see* anything in all that dark?"

Griffin clambered into the empty spot in front of his mom, settling in as the boat rocked impatiently. He didn't care one bit about Stella. He just wanted his dad back.

"To the aerie," Katherine said, and the boat shimmied into the current of mists. The belly of the boat was polished to a mirror shine so it reflected the black of space overhead and the mists passing fleetingly by. Katherine leaned forward, wrapping her arms around her son. "How'd you sleep?"

"Seems like all I've done is sleep, ever since we got here." Griffin's words were swallowed in a yawn.

Katherine chuckled. "Apparently you're not finished catching up yet."

Griffin hung on to her arms where they crisscrossed his collarbone. He was still reminding himself that this was real, that she was okay. Maybe he wasn't in such a hurry to get home after all. He eyed the lighthouse tower again, all alone at the edge of the mists.

"Mom?"

"Yes?" Katherine exhaled, leaning back again to let the breeze wash over her as the boat climbed steadily upward.

"How come there's never anyone in the tower, guarding the portal? Aren't they afraid the priests will come here and attack Caligo next?"

"Hmmmm. It seems like such delicate magic, what the Levitator and his fleet do, holding everything up."

Griffin turned in his seat, rounding his spine and fitting it against the boat's curved bow so he could watch his mom's face light up while she spoke.

"Their gift is fierce, though, too. Only the invited

can remain on Caligo. When Somni first invaded, the old Levitator did the unthinkable: He commanded his fleet to let the soldiers fall. This world doesn't need guards in the tower like Vinea or an alarm system like we have back home. No foreigner can survive on this side of the portal unbidden."

Griffin shuddered. He glanced over his shoulder at the aerie. It was a broad platform with a nestlike building at the center. The fleet went about their work, loose strands of spider silk bobbing in the air behind them. Griffin had dismissed them as silly children and kindly recluses practicing their magic in a blissed-out meditative state. But there was more to it that he hadn't counted on.

That's the thing about magic. It has a hard edge, sharp enough to carve right through a person if he isn't careful.

FI

FI SAT ON the edge of the aerie's broad platform, her feet dangling over nothing but air. As her legs swung back and forth, the mists swirled around her ankles, daring her to launch off the ground and into their playful currents.

But Fi was in no mood for dares.

She kicked at a curious tendril of mist, glaring at the vertical gardens across the span of stark white. The only thing better than being home, on Vinea, would be *there*, with the greenwitches. What little plant life could be found on Caligo was in those gardens, and it seemed to pull at her, beckoning across the space between floating islands. The greenwitches were over there having some sort of meeting. Some all-day kind of gathering. And they were ignoring her.

They had been ever since Fi and Griffin and his mom had been pulled through the portal in the lighthouse to Caligo. The Levitator had said the three of them were crucial to defeating Somni's priests, but all she'd done so far was sit around and wait. On second thought, maybe Fi was ready to jump off the edge to test the boundaries of the Levitator and his fleet's holding-every-single-thing-up power. Maybe then somebody would pay attention to her.

She wasn't even supposed to be here. While the resistance was fighting to win back their home world—battling the priests on Somni and storming the fort on Vinea to free the wildlands—she was stuck here, useless. And the people she ached to be with? The ones who seemed to have stepped out of legend right in front of her eyes?

They were ignoring her.

Ever since she'd first glimpsed the greenwitches, all she'd wanted was to be with them. There were twelve—more than she'd ever imagined might still be alive—all in one place and lighting up the mists with green magic flowing through their veins. Other than her great-aunt Una, Fi had never met another greenwitch. They were rare a hundred years ago, before the Somni invasion. And after? She'd heard that the priests had hunted down and killed every last one of them.

Yet here they were.

Fi had spent twenty-seven months on Somni as a spy, and while some of those days were full of intrigue and heart-in-your-throat terror, most of them passed painfully slowly. Watching this door, waiting for that person to come or go, and then biting her tongue for hours until she could report what she'd seen. And the worst part? She had to act like a servant. All the spies did if the resistance was going to stay hidden.

To pass the time while she scrubbed and dusted and polished, she told herself stories of the Vinea the resistance would bring back, teeming with life. She imagined greenwitches emerging from hiding deep in the wildlands and calling on the green magic to cleanse their world of Somnites for good.

She'd dreamed of that victory so many times, it was like a favorite memory playing over in her mind. But she'd never really believed it was possible. The greenwitches were gone. The resistance would have to find a way to beat back Somni without them.

Only they weren't *all* gone. Fi glared across the mists. They were here. Not fighting shoulder to shoulder with the resistance. Not ending the Somni occupation. If Fi had even an ounce of the green magic in her veins, she'd use up every last drop to win Vinea back. The only reason the priests had been able to colonize all those other worlds was that they'd used their mind control, and the best way to fight magic was with magic. The resistance needed the green-witches' help. And Fi couldn't even begin trying to convince them if they only ignored her.

Fi's thoughts were interrupted by a sudden movement in the distance. She hopped to her feet, squinting. There—past the gardens and the library that spiraled up into the mists, seemingly with no beginning and no end, almost as far away as the lighthouse at the edge of the city in the sky—a boat had left the little floating island where Griffin and his mom were staying and began winding slowly toward the aerie.

Fi paced back and forth along the edge of the platform. Katherine had invited her to stay with them, of course. But Fi wouldn't leave her spot opposite the gardens. She slept there, ate there, and swatted sullenly at the perky mists trying to draw her out of her gloom. The greenwitches might be ignoring her, but she wouldn't let them forget about her.

When the boat drew close, Fi waved and Griffin waved back, laughing at something Katherine said. As soon as they were near enough, he jumped from the boat onto the platform, and Fi stumbled out of his way, playfully shoving him back toward the edge. Katherine climbed up after her son, wrapping Fi in a hug.

"You'll stay with us tonight, won't you?" She'd asked that same question every day, so she must have already known the answer.

Fi shook her head, her lips twisting to the side. She wanted to say yes, so badly.

Katherine dropped her arms, fixing Fi with a sharp look. "You'll let me know if you change your mind?"

Fi nodded. She glanced over her shoulder at the fleet dashing back and forth, hurrying about the Levitator's business. She didn't like the idea that a kid younger than her was in charge. How'd he get so lucky? If Fi had all that power, she wouldn't waste it. She'd finish the priests. For good.

The people of Caligo looped their silver hair in intricate topknots and wore spider silk clothing that wound like spun sugar over their bodies. The elderly members of the fleet sat on fluffy white cushions, their eyes closed, like they were napping sitting up. Katherine insisted they were actually working their magic, holding up the observatory, the mews, the library, and all the people too. But Fi didn't trust it. How did they know *everybody* was covered? What if they *did* fall asleep? Or get bored? Or distracted? It didn't seem like a very good system. She preferred good old-fashioned dirt beneath her feet, thank you very much.

Melanie Crowder

And their skin? Fi shuddered. When a Caligion wanted to go unseen, you could walk right in front of one of them without knowing it. Griffin said there were animals on Earth who could do that same shifty thing. His encyclopedia voice took over as he rattled off details about cephalopods, whose skin changed to mimic the sea floor they glided over. He thought it was cool, but she didn't like it.

Fi walked with Griffin and his mom under the high roof of the nest, straight into the flurry of activity. The Levitator's attendant, a brusque woman named Leónie, stepped out of the shadows, her skin rippling as it shifted to reflect the glare of white mists behind her. She wore her pale hair twisted in ornate cones, and a long-legged silver spider perched on her shoulder.

Leónie held up a hand. "The Levitator can't see you now."

"But—" Katherine began.

"Why not?" Griffin said.

"He is in Sight."

"What does *that* mean?"

"Things are happening in the far-flung worlds that require his attention." Leónie brought her hands together, the pad of each finger meeting its opposite and pushing back. "He left a message for you."

The others leaned in, waiting for Leónie to finish that thought, but the woman seemed perfectly content to watch them squirm. She inspected the diagonal curve of her long fingernails and absently petted the spider that was slowly making its way down her arm, its many eyes fixed on the visitors.

"Well, what is it?" Fi finally blurted.

"Over the past few days, the Levitator has observed legions of soldiers led by Somnite priests moving through the portal from Somni to Vinea, marching without stopping. The thing you three were called to Caligo to do—it's happening." She looked down her nose. "You should go now, and make ready."

More soldiers? Fi ground her teeth together. Someone had to warn the resistance. That stupid Levitator had no business yanking her here when she should be on Vinea right now, fighting—

"Fionna?"

The voice came from behind Fi, and it stopped her thoughts, and her breath too. It wasn't anyone Fi recognized, but the sound trembled through her, awakening something deep inside. Her eyes drifted closed, and a flash of green lit the backs of her eyelids. She reached out and Griffin's hand was there to steady her. Fi blinked, shaking her head clear, then spun on her heel, her throat tight, a familiar ache in her chest. There, at the edge of the platform, one of the greenwitches waited beside an eager boat.

The same jumble of emotions that churned inside her played over Griffin's face. He squeezed her hand. "What are you waiting for? Go!"

3

FI

WHEN FI LEAPED out of the boat and into the vertical gardens, the ground dipped like a sponge beneath her feet, springing back into place when she stepped away. Fi gasped as the green rose up to meet her, spilling into her lungs and coursing through her blood. The entire island was made of plants. From the ground beneath her to the trellises that arced overhead and the glade of trees at its heart—all of it was green.

The only living architecture Fi had ever encountered was in the chapels on Vinea. They'd form whenever someone crossed over the threshold, only to dissolve into the jungle again once they'd left. But she'd heard of so many other kinds of living structures from before the Somni invasion—bridges and lookout towers, homes and schools. Fi rested her palm against sturdy vines that formed a thick pillar rising into the mists, bracing the more delicate plants that fountained off it.

The moss shifted beneath her feet, and Fi glanced over her shoulder as the woman who'd come to get her from the aerie approached. She wore an unreadable expression on her face and a dappled tunic trimmed at the knees in front and dipping to brush against her calves in the back.

Fi had half a mind to reach out and grab the woman's jaw, turning it side to side so she could examine the veins that cut across her forehead and along the cords of her neck. But she didn't need to. It wasn't the starlight glimmering off the greenwitch's skin, or the weight of Fi's wishing that made it true. The woman glowed, the green in her veins as bright as the new tips on an evergreen branch.

Fi looked down at the backs of her own hands. Veins cut across the tendons, pale green like all Vineans. Nothing special. Nothing magical. They didn't glow, not like a greenwitch.

The woman laid a hand on her chest. "You may call me Ness." She crossed under an ivy arch and gestured to the ground at her feet.

Fi knelt, plunging her fingers into the ground

cover for comfort. The mosses pressed against her palm in response, their tiny spores tilting toward her like miniature sunflowers chasing the sun. A shy smile crept over Fi's lips and she forgot for a moment to be nervous. She forgot to wonder why they'd called her here, or what might be happening back home.

The light shifted in the garden as the rest of the greenwitches approached the glade. They moved slowly, pausing before each footfall until the greenery rose to meet them. Their skin was almost as pale as the mists, their veins pulsing with bright green life. Each had shorn her hair at the chin, though age had stolen the luster from what had been rich yellow, orange, and red hues. Their faces bore deep wrinkles, and though no malice hid in the creases beside their eyes or in the set of their lips, their gazes did not fall softly on Fi.

Vines rose to form stools and the greenwitches sank with unconscious ease onto the plaited seats. Ness knelt in front of Fi, so their knees nearly touched. "Do you know why your aunt Ada stayed on Vinea but you were sent to Somni?"

Fi sat back in surprise. How did Ness know Aunt Ada? "The resistance told me it was because the priests needed kids to do some of their work."

"That is true." Ness pulled her upper lip through

her teeth. "But it's not the only reason. Surely you know that we would have fought to the end of everything to keep our children safe if there wasn't a good reason to send them into that danger."

Fi scowled. This was not how she'd imagined this moment going. Four days and four nights she had waited in the cold on that platform, watching the greenwitches and wishing to be among them. For what—a history lesson?

"There is so much about greenwitches that the people of Vinea have lost—things they've made themselves forget, in order to protect us. It used to be that the green magic was spoken of in all things. Everyone knew its workings, even if the magic didn't flow through their family tree." Ness paused. Her berry-red hair was laced with white, framing a round face with half-lidded eyes and a mouth that worked slowly, as if there were no need to hurry anything, ever. "So you wouldn't have heard, then, that the green magic skips a generation."

"It does?"

Ness watched Fi with a haunted look. There was something more behind her words, something Fi was supposed to understand. Ness lifted Fi's hand and turned it over. She placed a small plant with roots exposed to the air and gemlike leaves into Fi's palm.

"See here—" She pointed to where the tips of the roots had shriveled and dried. "This plant is dying. It has closed itself off to the water in the air. It won't survive much longer."

"Well, why don't you save it, then?"

Ness drew her hands back. "Why don't you?"

"But—" Fi protested. "I don't know how."

"Then I suppose it will die."

Fi groaned. "But I'm not a greenwitch. I can't."

"Try."

Fi cupped the plant in her hands. She could almost feel it, the way the tiny thing thirsted but couldn't bring itself to drink. She looked up at the women encircling her. Their faces were impassive, lofty and removed from the kneeling girl below. At least, that's how it seemed to Fi. Before she knew it, anger rose like a tide inside her, spilling over the levy that held it back. Her palms grew hot and damp.

But beneath the anger, something else nudged its way to the surface. Fi squeezed her eyes shut. Suddenly there it was, glowing against the backs of her eyelids: a faint image of the plant in throbbing green. The joints from bud to stem to root had sealed—she could *see* it with her eyes closed. All they needed was reopening, like sluice gates holding back a stream.

Fi blinked furiously. What was happening to her?

Sweat formed on her forehead. She closed her eyes again, wiggled her toes deeper into the moss, and just as Ness suggested, she tried.

She *pushed* against the joints, and, to her surprise, they opened. The little plant that had barely pulsed with green began to glow, beads of life speeding in and out of the roots, filtering through the stem and out to the tips of each leaf.

Fi opened her eyes. Ness was beaming. They all were beaming.

"Look," Ness prodded, and once again, she lifted Fi's arm. Just as it had within the tiny plant, green flowed through Fi's veins, bright as a thatch of newborn grass. The veins didn't glow, not like Ness's, but they were definitely brighter than before.

Fi stared at her arm as if it belonged to someone else. "I don't understand."

Ness tipped her head to the side. "If you had remained on our green world, your blood would have begun ripening in your eleventh year. This would have put you in grave danger. You would have been a fugitive for the rest of your life. We had to send you away to protect you, to slow the green waking within you."

"What do you mean, 'ripening'?"

"It happened to all of us, once, when we were

young. The green magic flares inside a person and grows to its full potential."

"Me?" Fi's voice was small. "You're saying I'm a greenwitch?"

Ness reached out and clasped both of Fi's hands. "We did the cruelest thing. For decades, we sent the children we suspected might have magic in their veins directly to the enemy. Like you, they were hidden in plain sight on Somni, unaware. We suspected that on that lifeless world, their magic would remain dormant until it was safe to return home."

Fi stared at the plant in her hands. Already, it seemed more plump, lifting its spears toward the mists that curled around them. *She* did that. She'd never done anything like that in her whole life! She should be thrilled, or proud, or something. Instead she squirmed, not sure she was entirely comfortable with this new version of herself.

"Fionna, if we haven't damaged you by holding back the green magic, and if your great-aunt Una is any indication, you should be very powerful indeed."

Fi dipped her chin and stared at Ness from beneath wary brows. Was she joking? Were the greenwitches making fun of her? The women dropped from the stools and came to congratulate Fi one at a time. They cupped her elbows in their palms and whispered welcomes over the glow that had begun to rise from the pale skin of her forearms.

Fi fought the urge to snatch her arms back. Something still wasn't right. "Why now?"

Ness sat back. "Excuse me?"

"Why am I here now? Why are you saying this today, and not two years ago, or four days ago when I got here? What do you know that I don't?"

A tight smile crept over Ness's lips. "We have come to a decision. It isn't enough anymore for us to remain here, carrying on our traditions. Too many have died. Too much has been lost." She exchanged a determined look with the other greenwitches. "We are ready to fight back."

Fi's heart slammed against her chest. "Then what are you waiting for? Let's go! The resistance needs you."

Ness chuckled. "Fionna, we're well aware of your bravery. But we're not sending you into danger again until you're strong enough not just to fight, but to win."

FI

FOR THEIR FIRST lesson, Ness took Fi to the observatory, where massive cone-shaped structures were trained on the stars at all times. But Fi wasn't there for the stars.

The observatory was the island farthest from the lighthouse and its sweeping beams. It was far from the gardens, too, where there was an abundance of green to distract Fi's senses. She sat beside Ness at the edge of the observatory's deck, swinging her feet over thin air. Behind them, the sky watchers went quietly about their business. Fi wedged her hands beneath her thighs, trying to convince her nerves to quit jangling.

If Ness noticed, she didn't let on. "The first thing to know about the green magic is that it's not something you have to search for. It's already inside you, waiting for the last frost to pass, and eager for the bloom."

Fi gulped. She didn't feel anything blooming inside her. Well, except maybe impatience. Her people were in the middle of a war they were inches from losing. Budding greenwitch or not, she belonged on Vinea, right now. Every day she wasted on Caligo, people died.

But Ness only continued her speech. "Even the smallest bit of life calls to us, though there is a limit to the green we can perceive. Greenwitches can't work with a seed or a clump of dried herbs—we need a sprout or even a single root clinging to life. We aren't gods. We can't create life."

Fi ground her teeth together. She wanted this—she did. A greenwitch's power was more than she'd ever dreamed for herself. But now? The timing couldn't have been worse.

"Your task today is to quiet your mind and invite the green in."

Fi suppressed a groan. The very last thing her mind had ever been was quiet.

5

GRIFFIN

GRIFFIN STOOD AT the edge of their little island, watching for whatever Leónie's warning might mean and chafing the skin of his upper arms to warm them. He and his mom had been offered some of that spider silk clothing the people wore on Caligo, but even though their stolas were hopelessly stained, they were at least a little warmer. At this point, Griffin would give just about anything for a pair of jeans and a hoodie. And some socks. Thick, wool socks.

Leónie hadn't moved since she practically shoved him and his mom back into their boat. The Levitator came to stand beside her in the glossy feather cloak he wore to greet newcomers. They waited at the very edge of the aerie's platform, and together they stared intently at the lighthouse. The Levitator was smaller than his attendant and younger than Griffin, but the boy thrummed with power. His hands were clasped behind his back, and even from a distance, Griffin could see him wring and twist them when he thought no one was looking.

The lighthouse thrust into the sky, the white-washed bricks nearly blending into the mists. Griffin peered at the bank of windows beneath the bright red roof, squinting for a better look at the lens. He could just make out the brass fittings between panels, and the slightly greenish hue of the glass.

Griffin's breath caught. Something wasn't right. He jumped to his feet. The lens wasn't turning. It always turned, night and day, unless—

He began to tremble, not unlike the hum that was surely rattling through the tower at that very moment. "Mom! Come here, quick."

Katherine drifted outside, answering without looking up from the book in her hands. "Hmmm?"

"The portal—it's opening!"

Katherine's head snapped up. She tucked the book under her arm and reached out to clasp her son's hand. In the tower, a dark form blinked into being in the lantern room, a silhouette against the pale glass. Slowly, the giant Fresnel lens began to swivel on its pedestal again, winking as the eight panels rotated, catching and releasing the light. The figure in the tower seemed to shake himself and look around. He stepped outside onto the balcony, bracing his weight against the iron rails and taking in the floating city of Caligo.

Griffin gasped, and Katherine's grip tightened, her book falling to the floor, forgotten. Griffin knew that stance—he'd seen it a million times back home, when his dad leaned on the gallery railing, watching the ocean beyond the headland.

"Dad!" Griffin shouted across the expanse that separated them, and Philip jerked at the sound of his voice.

It had only been a few days since they'd been separated, but it had been a restless, uneasy separation. Griffin had hardly been able to sleep nights, between the wonder at having his mother suddenly returned to him and the worry for his dad back on Somni.

His excitement was quickly dampened. "Something must be wrong. Why would Dad be *here*?"

"Come on." Katherine stepped into the boat, pulling Griffin with her. "We'll know soon enough."

"To the tower," Griffin said, and the boat lurched away from its perch, dancing along the currents of mist like a leaf bobbing in a stream. He leaned forward, nearly tipping the craft end over end in his eagerness.

Melanie Crowder

The boats always sped along the currents of mist—Griffin knew that. But this time it seemed like an undertow dragged at the hull, making the trip from their little island to the lighthouse agonizingly slow. When they finally floated up to the top of the tower, Philip threw his leg over the railing, leaning out over nothing and reaching for them. The boat sidled alongside the gallery and Philip jumped in.

The Fenn family fell into a heap in the boat's belly, arms wrapped around one another, gleeful laughter spilling from their lips. They could deal later with whatever had gone wrong to bring Philip to them. For now, they were together, and nothing else mattered.

The boat didn't seem to mind that its passengers weren't paying any attention to where it carried them; it responded to the fleet's call, climbing obediently toward the aerie. The mists surrounded them, offering a little privacy for the tender reunion. Or perhaps they simply wished to join in the celebration.

Philip pulled back at last, a broad smile stretching across his grizzled cheeks. "It's been horrible, knowing you were together and I was missing it—missing *you*!"

Katherine drew a hand along a nearly healed scrape behind his ear. "You're certainly looking better than the last time I saw you."

Philip ducked his chin to kiss her palm.

Griffin flushed, but he couldn't drag his eyes away. "Dad, but—how did you know we were here, on Caligo? You told us to go to Earth. We were supposed to be at home."

Philip drew Katherine down to sit beside him, tucking his arm firmly around her waist. "I meant to go home, but the portal to this world opened instead, and before I knew what was happening, I was yanked here." He winked, reaching to pull Griffin to his other side. "Kind of like you, I'm guessing?" The boat tipped at an alarming angle as all three Fenns piled in the stern.

Katherine glanced toward the aerie, and the meddling Levitator. "But why did you leave Somni so soon? We assumed it would be weeks and weeks until you finished your work, and until it was safe to leave the caves."

Philip shrugged. "I thought so too. But the priests left Somni. Completely. They abandoned their home world, taking all their soldiers with them, to who knows where. It would make sense if they traveled to Vinea, I suppose, to tamp down the rebellion there."

"Do the greenwitches know?" Griffin interrupted. "And Fi?"

"Who?" Philip asked.

"You remember, my friend—the girl who knocked out that priest who had us all trapped in the chapel back on Somni," Griffin said. "She's here on Caligo with us, not that she's happy about it."

"Wait—did you say greenwitches? I thought the priests wiped them out decades ago."

"That's a long story," Katherine said. "First—the priests left Somni? How is that possible?"

"Yeah, well, *that* was a surprise the Somnite rebels weren't expecting. I made as many pendants as I could and they passed them out to anyone left in the city. I even made a surplus, for the soldiers. The rebels hope to be able to save them, though the Vinean resistance was reluctant, to say the least, to go along with that plan, after all they'd suffered at the soldiers' hands." Philip hugged Katherine and Griffin tighter. "My part was finished. So I left as soon as I could, to come home to you two."

Beside him, Katherine's face was drawn in a decided frown. "They simply left? After everything—brainwashing their own citizens and stealing people from other worlds to siphon off their dreams so they could lord over all eight worlds? It doesn't make sense." She shook her head slowly. "We're missing something."

Griffin looked between his parents, unease

seeping in like a wave breaching the walls of a sand castle, leaving nothing but soggy lumps in its place. Whatever happened next, his family had done their part. They should be able to go home, together, at last. So why couldn't he believe that?

GRIFFIN

T HE LEVITATOR HELD meetings in the very center of the aerie, under the nest's lofty roof. The three Fenns kneeled before him, waiting. Unlike the rest of the Caligions, he was bald as an egg. The spider silk garment that wrapped over his torso curved out at his slim shoulders like the sloping petal of a calla lily. He perched on a feather pillow, the picture of serenity. That is, until he began chewing at a corner of his lip like a kid with a crayon that keeps veering out of the lines.

"Mr. Fenn," the Levitator began. "We are so glad you've joined us in our floating city."

"Did I have a choice?" Philip muttered.

Katherine jabbed an elbow into his ribs. "What

my husband means to say is, thank you for reuniting our family. We are grateful."

A man with a beaklike nose and hair twisted into a silver beehive carefully lowered a tray of wobbling egg cups to the floor. The Levitator leaned forward, offering an eggshell full of some inky liquid to each of the Fenns.

Philip took a sip. His tongue worked in his mouth as his eyebrows climbed toward his hairline. "Yes." He tried swallowing again. "Very grateful."

Griffin lifted the cup to his lips, taking the tiniest sip possible. A shudder rippled through him. He'd gotten used to the way food on Caligo tasted over the past few days, but the texture—it was like swallowing a squished grape, sweet, veined, and more than a little slimy.

The Levitator made a sweeping gesture with his arm, and as it passed beyond the edge of his spun silk garment, his skin shifted to mimic the white of the mists and the steel gray of the ceiling. "The old Levitator did not approve of meddling in other worlds. His only exception was saving the green-witches as they were being taken from Vinea to Somni, to their deaths. He couldn't sit by and watch the slaughter of fellow magic workers."

Griffin scowled. Of course the greenwitches deserved saving. But didn't everybody? Why hadn't the old Levitator saved Griffin's dad when he was kidnapped by the priests? Or his mom, all those years before?

The Levitator reached for the refreshments, a gleam lighting up his eyes. "I plan to deal differently with our sister worlds. I don't think Caligo should only watch at a distance while others suffer."

"Again," Katherine said, "we thank you."

The Levitator topped off each of their cups, never mind that not one of them had asked for refills. "There is a Sight that comes with this role. I can only see so far—a little ways into the portal to each world. I guess you already know the Somnite army has been moving."

"Yes," Philip said.

The Levitator tugged at the fabric over his knees. He squirmed in his seat. "There's more. Some of the priests went to Earth."

"What?" Griffin scrambled to his feet. Of all eight worlds, only Stella and Earth had resisted Somni occupation. Keeping Somni out of Earth was the whole reason the Society of Lighthouse Keepers existed, and why their leader, Dr. Hibbert, had betrayed the Fenns.

The Levitator held up a hand. His voice squeaked a little when he continued, at odds with the whole sage-in-the-sky thing he tried to pull off. "That's not the worst part. By the time the priests get back to the portal, they are shepherding people from Earth with them. People under their control."

"No!" Katherine cried.

"But if the priests aren't even on Somni anymore, they don't need to steal any more dreamers. Why would they . . . ?" Griffin trailed off at the dismay on his parents' faces, at whatever they'd clearly guessed that he didn't yet understand.

"Soldiers." Philip's voice was hard. "Earth has no natural protection from the priests' powers of mind control. One thing we're very good at, though, is war. Trained soldiers falling easily under Somni's control—of course the priests would look to Earth to raise another army."

Dread coiled inside Griffin. "But—I took the block off the lens, so Mom and I could go home. That means I'm the reason they could travel to Earth. I did this."

Katherine brushed a wayward curl out of his eyes. "No, Griffin. The evil of others is only ever their own fault."

"I'm so sorry." The Levitator rushed to explain,

his words spilling together. "I should have seen this sooner. So many of the priests were traveling to Vinea to meet the battle there—I didn't notice the first few who went to Earth instead. All I know is—they go in, one at a time. And when they come back through, each one brings dozens of people from Earth with him."

For the first time since Griffin had arrived on Caligo, the Levitator seemed like the kid he was. Not some all-powerful magic worker, just a scared kid.

Philip jumped up. "The alarm would've sounded. The Keepers *have* to be on alert."

"But they have no leader," Katherine said, "and we know how long it takes that gaggle to come to any decision."

"Somebody would have called the Coast Guard for help, at least. We have to believe that." Philip yanked at the ends of his hair. "*How* did we miss this?"

"There has to be a way to stop them." Griffin's voice sounded feeble in his own ears.

"If we find a way to guard the people of Earth from the priests' mind control, we could stop them from kidnapping anyone else. We need to limit the damage they can do." Katherine began to pace the small room. "The malva vine won't work. We'd drain

Vinea's supply before we covered the West Coast. Same with Somni's sjel tree essence. There's no way it could shield everyone on Earth."

Philip nodded. "We'd need a way to reach millions of people quickly."

Katherine spun to face the Levitator. "Do the mists protect Caligions? Could we somehow bring a sample home and let it loose in Earth's atmosphere?"

The Levitator shook his head, his lips clamped into a thin line. "I'm sorry, but no. We resist the priests by never letting them near us. Our people travel this world freely. We have very few restrictions in our society. But the boats will not carry any citizen of Caligo within earshot of the lighthouse. It is forbidden."

"Mom!" Griffin caught the edge of her sash as she swept by. "What about Maris? You told me the ocean's song guards the people's minds."

Katherine nodded slowly. "It does."

"Could it protect Earth, too?"

Philip scraped his palm across the stubble covering his jawline. "Possibly. It's a good idea. But we'd have to find a way to get it from Maris to Earth. And how would we even capture something like a song?"

The Levitator shook his head. "I don't have any of the answers you need. But the Levitators have always watched the portals, observing the seven other worlds and writing down what they saw. Those records are kept in our library, the greatest on any world. If anyone outside Maris knows the answer to your question, you'll find it there."

GRIFFIN

THE LIBRARY WAS beyond the gardens, past the mews and markets, a narrow spiral standing alone in the mists. As the Fenns' boat swung alongside one of the narrow platforms, Philip leaped out, turned, and reached back for Katherine and Griffin.

A broad bookshelf lined the platform. It stretched well over Griffin's head, and was fitted with wheeled ladders for rolling back and forth. He grabbed on to one, gave it a push, and watched as it careened toward the edge and stopped suddenly with a bang. The next floor up held another wall of shelves, set at a slight angle from the first, with its own ladders ready to slide back and forth at the librarian's whim. Above that one was another, set again at an angle, and another, and another, so the bookshelves spun upward until they were swallowed by the mists.

Griffin leaned over the edge, peering down. More shelves spiraled below—he counted six and a half stories down before they dropped out of sight. The shelves seemed to sway slightly, twisting like one of those wooden wind spinners people hung off their porches back home.

The bookshelf directly in front of Griffin was empty of books, its only occupant a sign that read RING BELL. Griffin stepped up and pressed the shiny button. The tinny *ding* didn't seem like it would travel very far at all, but then something moved, far below.

Something big.

It fell away from the backside of a bookshelf, and then it swiveled, catching the air under huge wings to break its fall. A beat after the first creature dropped off, a second fell away two stories up. And a third. Suddenly the gaps between books shifted in front of Griffin's nose—what he'd thought were brass fittings for the shelves pulled back, revealing talons as big as his torso. The creature's wings snapped open, flattening Griffin's hair over his ears.

He yelped. Philip gripped Katherine around the waist and pulled Griffin against him, his knees bent to absorb any more shocks of wind. The creature peeled away from the shelves, twisting in an airborne dance.

"Magnificent," Katherine breathed.

"What *are* those?"

"I have no idea." Philip relaxed his grip, a little.

"Look!" Griffin pointed far below, where the creatures were rising steadily, darting in and out of layers of mist. "They're coming back."

They settled into a loose formation, headed straight toward the Fenns. Their giant wings pumped, mud-black as the basalt rocks beneath the lighthouse.

"Hold on!" Philip shouted above the gusts of wind.

Just when it seemed like the creatures would crash into the library, all but one pulled up, gripping the backs of the shelves with wicked claws and hanging like a colony of enormous bats. The largest one swooped behind the Fenns, steadily pumping its wings. A man peeked around the side of the bat's furry chest, his skin rippling to mirror the currents of air swirling in the wake of those massive wings.

"You rang?"

Griffin gulped. "You're the librarian?"

The man adjusted his spectacles. "That's me. And you're the Earth folk our young Levitator is sheltering."

"Yes," Katherine said, clearing her throat and stepping forward. "And he sent us here—we have urgent business."

Melanie Crowder

"I see. How can I help you?"

"We need to look through everything you have on Maris."

"And quickly, if you can. Please." Philip tacked on that last part after a pointed look from his wife.

The librarian nodded curtly. "That would be twenty-three stories up from where you stand now. Hop on." Three of the batlike creatures dropped away from the shelves, twisting until they were belly-up to the platform, their giant claws gripping the edge inches from Griffin's toes. Their black eyes blinked, waiting.

Katherine scooted her toes to the very edge of the platform.

"Mom!" Griffin protested. "Seriously?"

"Make a circle with your arms," the librarian instructed. "Lock your hands together and hold on tight."

"I'll be *fine*," Katherine said, tossing a devilish smile over her shoulder. The bat beneath her swiveled, tucked its wings tight to its sides, and flung itself up through the open circle of her arms. Katherine was swept away in a spiral of black and a rustle of wings.

Griffin's heart seemed to beat in his throat. The air pummeled his eardrums and the mists curled around him, trying to soothe his frayed nerves. A moment later, Katherine was back, floating in the air beside the librarian, astride the bat's shoulders. Griffin backed away from the edge.

"Come on!" Katherine called. "It's Caligo. Even if you fell, you wouldn't *fall*."

He *knew* that. He wasn't afraid of bats—at least, not normal-sized ones. Every now and then, one got stuck in the lantern room of the lighthouse back home, flapping pitifully at the windows, trying to get out. He and his dad had always worked together to set them free again without hurting them. But these bats were the size of bears—with wings.

Griffin screwed his eyes shut and held out his arms like a human basketball hoop. Before he knew it, he was hugging a furry chest, the mists breaking over his face like a river over a boulder. Water streamed out the corners of his eyes and his skin rippled in the wind.

Then, suddenly, Griffin's stomach lurched and his hair flopped into his face. He wasn't flying through the air, so maybe he hadn't plunged into the mists after all. Griffin cracked one eye open.

"You're okay." It was his mother's voice, close beside him. Calm and reassuring. His bat hovered right beside his mom's. And then the one carrying his dad settled a wingspan away.

Melanie Crowder

Without another word, the librarian shot up and the Fenns' three bats followed after. They didn't seem to have an in-between gear—it was either full stop or full speed ahead. And they weren't really bats. The part of Griffin's brain that wasn't screaming in gleeful terror noticed that their flight was more direct than that. Less flitting, more swooping.

"Level thirty-seven," the librarian announced. "Ring the bell again when you're ready for a ride back down."

Griffin's bat pulled up his claws and reared back, dropping him onto the platform right-side up beside his parents. Griffin released his white-knuckled grip on the bat's fur, and with a *whoosh*, the creature was gone. Katherine wistfully tracked their spirals below.

"Right." Philip looked like he'd been through a wind tunnel. He raked his fingers through his hair, trying to coax it to lay flat again. "The Levitator said to look for the books with embossed green spines."

Griffin tore his gaze away from the sky and scanned the shelves in front of him. "There!" A row of books as tall as his arm were wrapped in green paper that shimmered like a peacock feather. Each spine was inscribed with a single, painstakingly lettered word.

"One for each of the Levitators," Katherine observed.

"So they just spy on everybody and then write about it?"

Philip pulled the ladder toward him and balanced on the first rung while he handed down one volume for each of them. "I guess we'll find out."

When the Fenn family finally stumbled home for the evening, their eyes were strained, their fingertips paper-cut, and their bellies grumbling. The librarian, seeing their book-bleary eyes, had asked the bats to ferry them straight to their little island. When they arrived, a meal of strangely shaped and colored boiled eggs, along with a crisp bread that was more air pockets than anything else waited for them.

Philip swallowed a yawn, dragging the pads of his fingers across his eyelids. Griffin plopped onto the ground and Katherine settled beside him.

"Thank goodness the priests never gained access to that library. Can you even imagine . . ." Her voice trailed off, but the grim set of her mouth said more than enough. She drew the stack of books they'd brought back with them toward her.

Griffin wriggled under her arm, looking up into his mom's face until she blinked back the memories and her eyes focused on him again. She squeezed Griffin's shoulder, gave a little shake of her head, and began flipping through the pages of the book in front of her.

Philip eyed the platter of food reluctantly. "I suppose we should eat something."

Griffin didn't want to even guess what sort of flying creature might have hatched the purple speckled egg on the plate in front of him. He plugged his nose and shoved one into his mouth.

"So. What do we know?" Katherine talked around her bites, the skin at the bridge of her nose crinkling as she swallowed. "The people of Maris—"

"Marisians," Philip added.

"Right. Their world warmed much more quickly than ours. Centuries ago, the oceans rose, drowning the land. The people built fleets of ships with sophisticated rain collection mechanisms, water gardens, and navigational systems. They learned to live like nomads, drawing everything they needed from the sea. As time passed, their bodies adapted to the harsh conditions."

Griffin jumped in. "They've got huge lungs for diving, thick skin like sharks, and a layer of blubber that keeps them warm in the ocean."

"Each of the eight worlds has some sort of magic, and on Maris, it's the song." Katherine hummed absently as she flipped through the book in her lap.

"There was some mention of *other* things the song could do besides guard the people's minds, but the entry was vague, to say the least. Something about how the Marisians and the ocean's song could enter into a kind of communion—not unlike the Somnites and their sjel trees."

Philip settled in beside them. "Well, the song may have protected the Marisians' minds when Somni invaded, but the soldiers still outnumbered and overwhelmed them. The priests stole their boats and with it, their way of life."

Outside, the mists turned a lavender hue, then a muted silver. Prickles inched up Griffin's arms as memory grabbed hold of him. It had been like this often, in the years before Katherine disappeared, the three of them arranged around the fire in the sitting room, each lost in a book, but together, and quietly content. Griffin swallowed past a lump in his throat. He'd missed this. Even with everything going wrong, even with Somni's priests a bigger threat than they'd ever been, he was grateful for one evening like it used to be.

Katherine took a sip of the fuchsia liquid in front of her, swallowing with a grimace. "We won't know if the song will work on Earth like it does on Maris until we bring it home and find out."

"*If* we can bring it home. How would we even *do* that?"

"Right. It's easy enough to snip off a length of malva vine and carry the plant with you through the portal. It's not so easy with something like a song."

"So what—we travel to Maris on a hunch? We go willingly into a world with soldiers and priests everywhere, all in the hopes that the song will do what we need it to? What if the Marisians don't want to help us? What if everything goes right—we get through the portal, make contact with the Marisians, and then they turn us over to the soldiers?"

Katherine sucked on her lower lip. "Do we have a choice?"

The room fell quiet. A swarm of bright yellow birds with long, rippling tail feathers circled the floating island and sped away again like pebbles out of a slingshot. The mists swirled and spun in their wake, rustling the pages of the scattered books.

"We have to try," Philip said, though he didn't look half as certain as he sounded. "We'd never make a single move if we waited to have answers to every possible question."

Griffin leaned against his mom's shoulder. It wasn't over for the Fenn family after all, and maybe it never would be. But he wouldn't let them get separated onto different worlds, not again. If one of them was leaving, they were all going. Together.

At length, Katherine spoke. "If we could free the Marisians, we would. We have to trust that they'll do the same for us."

Griffin sat up and flipped to the back of his book. "I saw something about making contact when we first get there. It's sort of like a warning. Here." He dragged a finger down the page. "'Since the portal first opened, a chain of rudimentary whistles have been kept in the tower, that any visitor to Maris may announce their arrival. Only the welcome will be permitted to proceed beyond the lighthouse.'"

Philip blew out a tight breath. "We'll just have to hope we're welcome, then."

Griffin clambered to his feet with a yawn. "I have to tell Fi we're leaving. She needs to know about the soldiers taken from Earth. She deserves to hear that they are headed straight for Vinea."

"Okay," Katherine said. "But be quick. We're leaving for Maris as soon as we're done here."

8

FI

D ON'T LOOK DOWN. Fi balanced on a single leaf, her toes curled away from the ragged edge while Ness watched from the solid ground of the gardens. Solid as anything on Caligo, anyway.

The leaf was only as big as Fi's feet. If she moved in any direction, she'd be stepping onto thin air. Sure, the fleet was always around to keep people from falling. But Fi didn't like putting her life into the hands of strangers.

"Concentrate," Ness said, loudly enough that her voice carried across the space between them. "You can do this."

Sweat began to trickle down Fi's spine. It itched. She wanted to reach back and wipe it away, but if she twisted like that, she'd fall for sure.

Ness held a stack of the broad leaves. Her face blank, she tossed the topmost one over the edge. It floated, lazing downward. Without any ground to land on, it kept falling, growing smaller and paler as it drifted through the mists.

Fi wiped a trail of sweat out of her eyes. She was supposed to hop across the leaves like stepping stones, but no one was going to magick them into place between her and the garden. She had to do it. As if she could—as if that was even possible.

Ness lifted another leaf from the stack. She drew her hand back.

"Stop!" Fi shouted. "You're going too fast. I can't—"

"You can." Ness's voice was as calm as ever. She flung the leaf into the air, and like the last, it began its tilting fall. "Reach out. Let the green in you call to the green in it." The leaf continued to drop. "Listen. Can you hear it? Can you feel it beneath your skin?"

Fi screwed her eyes shut. All she could sense was frustration, building like a thunderstorm inside her. She couldn't do this. Ness and the others were wrong, and they were wasting their time on her. She wasn't a greenwitch; she was a spy. She should be on Vinea right now, working for the resistance.

Eb had taken a blow that was meant for her. He'd died, for what—so she could mess around on Caligo while the real fighting raged on Vinea? Hot air flared Fi's nostrils. Her eyes snapped back open.

Ness held a third leaf between her fingertips, her eyebrow cocked, asking a question neither one of them needed her to voice. She opened her fingers and the leaf fell, leaving only five left in the stack. If Fi was going to set them in the gap between her and the gardens, she'd better figure out how before they were all gone.

"Just—wait!" Fi jammed her fists against her eyes so she didn't have to watch that leaf swish downward. *Shut up. Shut up.* The frustration didn't go anywhere, but the rest of the noise in her head dimmed a little. *Breathe.*

Anger simmered along her skin. This was never going to work.

But then the wind shifted, wafting the smell of the musky blooms in the vertical gardens past her. There was houseleek, and rockfoil, and lungwort spilling over stout containers, and climbers winding up narrow trellises, gathering honeybees and hummingbirds from the farthest stretches of the city in the sky. The scent of growing things put her at ease, and her breaths finally slowed, the hammering in her ears fading.

The smell hung in the air until the anger was gone too, until the leaf beneath her feet seemed wide as a field of clover. Mist coated Fi's skin. The chill breeze teased the ends of her hair. She could feel it all. And then, suddenly, there was something else. It wasn't a noise. It was somehow behind the other sounds and beyond anything she could touch.

With her eyes closed, life bloomed all around Fi, pulsing green like an army of marching ants. The leaf beneath her feet glowed, and the veins winding through Ness, and the tangle of the vertical gardens, and the leaves in the greenwitch's hands, and the next one that dropped away from the rest.

Stop.

Fi's eyes shot open.

The leaf hung in midair, unhindered by the mists or the breeze or, apparently, gravity. A faint glow, paler green than the greenwitches', rose from Fi's skin.

"You don't have to shout, you know." A wry smile curved Ness's lips.

"I didn't shout. I just thought—wait. I *did* that, didn't I?"

"The green did that," Ness corrected. "You asked. Well, you demanded, and it obliged. Try again. But gentler this time."

Fi closed her eyes and the pulsing trails of green life flared once more to light. She didn't know how she'd made that leaf stop its fall. She had no idea *how* it worked at all.

Help me?

"More specific," Ness instructed.

Up?

The leaf began to float upward, like one of the fleet's boats, until the edges brushed against Fi's fingertips. She crouched down, setting it on the air in front of her. She looked up into Ness's face, questioning.

"Again."

So she tried a second time, and a third, until the leaves filled in the gap between Fi and the gardens. The mists swirled through the gardens, rustling the needles high in the larch trees into a smattering of applause.

Ness nodded approvingly. "The only thing standing between you and the full power of the green magic is yourself."

Ness didn't know Fi very well, not yet. She probably hadn't even meant to phrase that last bit of encouragement like a dare. But a dare was all Fi heard. Her face grew hot and her mouth clamped shut. She lifted her chin and stepped across the air with nothing but a trail of wafer-thin leaves to keep her from falling.

9

FI

FI'S NEXT LESSON was a variation of the last. This time, rather than calling the plants to her, Ness instructed Fi to ask that they lift her high above the gardens. So she approached the ring of wispy larches with her question. In answer, the trees bent gladly toward her, and she hopped from one bough to the next, rising upward in a languid spiral. The view from the crown was dizzying, the islands dim shadows floating above and far below Fi's perch.

When Ness told Fi to calm her nerves or quiet her mind, it never worked. But up in the canopy, with the wind whipping the sleeves of her stola, the tang of pine in her nose, and the rough bark beneath her bare feet, Fi's worries slipped away. She didn't need to go looking for the green, it was simply there, in every fluttering leaf, in the cascade of life in the gardens below, in the air that flowed through her lungs.

"Ness!"

Fi startled, crouching low to the branch beneath her and wrapping her arms around the narrow trunk. The oldest greenwitch stood below, a withered woman named Val whose veins had already begun to dim. She beckoned frantically, shouting again. "Ness, come down from there. Quick!"

Fi and Ness scurried out of the tree. When they reached the ground, Val herded them toward the boats, her face grim. "We've been in contact with the resistance. Soldiers have been pouring through the portal into Vinea. They burned through the wildlands and stole the children we hid on Somni—the ones we think will become greenwitches."

"*No.*" It was barely above a whisper. "But how? Why?"

"We don't know—not what the priests want from them, or how the girls were found. Maybe their veins began to glow when they returned home, and it made them easy to single out."

Ness frowned. "And if the same happens to Fi when we take her through the portal?"

The rest of the women emerged from the gardens, encircling Val like the petals of a pine cone around its core. When two or three greenwitches stand near, the glow of their magic brightens the space between them. But when a dozen come together, the light changes—the air becomes charged like a sky split by thunder, and pale as the moment before a twister dips out of the clouds. It's why the greenwitches were so easily hunted down when Somni invaded. It's why Fi and the rest of the children were in such danger on Vinea, where the green pulsing through the wildlands nurtured the magic within them.

Val's voice trembled when she spoke, but not because of fear. It was age that shook her, that rattled the truth loose. "We're going to lose Vinea if we don't act quickly."

"I need more time. Fi isn't ready."

Val pursed her lips. "We simply don't have it."

"Now? We're leaving now?" It was what Fi had longed to hear. It was all she wanted, to return home to Vinea. But— "I need to say goodbye to Griffin. I need to thank Katherine."

"There isn't time."

"After everything we've been through, I can't just disappear. I need to tell him that—"

"Fionna. If we had even an hour to spare, we'd use that time to teach you, to somehow prepare you for the war we're sending you into." Ness bit her lip, and what Fi saw on the greenwitch's face caused a seed of worry to burrow into her.

"We give her the word to defend herself," Val said. "Only that. And then we leave."

Ness nodded, her eyes wide. She crouched until her eyes were level with Fi's. "Listen, and watch." The next time her voice sounded, it was deep in Fi's mind.

Shield me?

Ness's words reverberated through the gardens. The ring of stools collapsed, the vines untwining quick as writhing snakes. The vertical gardens trembled, then collapsed as, branch by branch, leaf by leaf, Ness was hidden from view.

"Ask!" Ness shouted over the whipping air.

Fi wet her lips. *Shield me?*

Instantly, she found herself in the eye of a second storm. The gardens were destroying themselves, bit by bit, to answer her call. Every last ounce of green in the city in the sky rushed through her. For the first time since she'd felt the green magic inside her, a thrill chased down Fi's skin.

Maybe it didn't matter that she didn't know enough, that she wasn't half as powerful as this fight needed her to be. The green was strong. So much stronger than she'd ever dared to dream.

FI

FI TOOK HER place beside Ness in the lighthouse tower. Greenwitches surrounded her on the watch room landing and lined the stairway leading to the lantern room, ready for the moment the portal opened.

Ness held up a tunic for Fi, who stepped out of her worn stola and lifted her arms over her head. The tunic slid over her skin, dropping past her torso with a shiver. She turned to one side, then the other, relishing the way the supple fabric brushed against her thighs. From one angle, the leaflike plates seemed as green as an evergreen bough. From another, they gleamed almost silver, like mosses dripping off tired branches.

"Thank you," she whispered. She stared down at

her arms, where a tiny glow touched the mists hovering around her. She bit her lip. "Do you think when I get home I'll glow like a greenwitch should?"

A frown tugged at Ness's mouth. "We don't really understand how your time on Somni altered the way the green works in you. You're different, it's true. But you're one of us, all the same."

Fi glanced back over her shoulder, out the watch room window, to the little floating island where Griffin and his mom were staying. She wished she could have seen Griffin one last time. She wished she could have gotten another one of Katherine's hugs. Maybe then she'd feel a little more like she was ready for whatever waited for her on the other side of the portal.

The lens groaned as it stopped turning. The greenwitch at the front of the line stepped up to the glass. Her tunic fell like plates of armor across her torso, and she stared forward, unblinking, as the curved brick walls of the tower began to shake.

Some of the women hadn't been home to Vinea in decades. Fi had only been away a little more than two years. But what if when she crossed over, the Vinea she remembered was gone? What if the resistance had already been defeated?

Fi ground her teeth together as the first greenwitch's tunic began to shimmer, the edges going translucent before she was sucked through the portal. The woman behind her stepped forward and then she, too, was gone. The line shrank until Fi and Ness were the only greenwitches left in the lantern room.

Fi eyed the Levitator, trying not to flinch while she waited for him to send her through the portal. The glass spun in front of her, beautiful and terrible at the same time. She had half a mind to jump through herself and take her chances. "Just get it over with already."

He actually smirked.

Ness grimaced. "What she means to say is, *Thank you.*"

"Yeah. That," Fi mumbled.

"The child and I go through together."

The Levitator nodded. "Does she know?"

Ness's eyes grew wide. She didn't answer.

He spoke again, this time locking eyes with Fi. "Does the girl know she's the one you've been waiting for?"

Shock swept the impatience from Fi's mind. She opened her mouth to ask what he meant—who was waiting for her? And why? But that familiar feeling of her insides being yanked to the outside eclipsed everything else. Light flared, and then suddenly everything went dark.

GRIFFIN

GRIFFIN GRIPPED THE edges of the boat as it lurched away from the platform, shimmying into the mists that swept toward the vertical gardens. He was scared for Fi—he wouldn't put it past her to do something rash when she heard about the soldiers from Earth headed to Vinea. She'd do anything to save her home world.

He banged his palms against the wood. "Come on, can't you go any faster?"

A gust of wind ruffled the sleeves of his stola, wafting a flotilla of airborne spiders overhead, silver against the black of space. Griffin ducked, wincing as a few of their parachute trails snagged in his hair. When the boat finally pulled up to the gardens, he didn't leap out as he'd planned. Instead, he gripped the sides of the boat, astonished. The gardens were a wreck, the trellises collapsed, and the trees naked of their leaves.

There was no one in sight, not anywhere. Had Fi left? Without even saying goodbye? Griffin stepped gingerly out of the boat and onto the uneven ground. It looked like the floating island had been hit by a tornado. Whatever *life* had held the place together was missing. The plants seemed to droop, flat as day-old soda. And that, more than anything else, convinced him—the greenwitches were gone.

It hit Griffin like a brick. He couldn't remember the last thing he'd said to Fi, but he knew it wasn't anything like what he would have said if he'd known that would be the last time they ever spoke. Years ago, after his mom's funeral, after all the relatives whose names he could barely remember had boarded airplanes back to the distant corners of the country they'd come from, Griffin would lay awake at night, trying to remember what had been the last thing he'd said to his mom. Had he held her tight enough? Had she *known* how wholly he loved her?

The thought had tortured him, all the long years before he'd discovered that Katherine was still alive, imprisoned on another world. He'd sworn that he would never feel that way again, that he'd tell people what they meant to him every chance he got. But this one had snuck up on him. How much Fi meant to Griffin had snuck up on him.

And now it was too late.

When the boat dropped Griffin back home, the Levitator was perched on a pillow in the center of the room, his attendant Leónie hovering over his right shoulder.

"She's gone!" Griffin's voice broke. "You should have told me. You could have given me the chance to say goodbye." He kicked the wall, his foot punching a jagged hole through the woven mat. Griffin looked up, sheepish. But instead of scolding, his parents came to stand beside him; his dad's arm dropped onto his shoulder and his mom's wrapped around his waist.

"We deserved to know," Katherine said.

The Levitator sat back in surprise, and his palms opened, cupping pools of mist. "I don't know what you expected me to do—the greenwitches left quickly when they heard. You can understand why, I'm sure."

"Look," Griffin said, his frustration spilling over. "You have to do more." Fi was headed straight into danger and he couldn't shake the feeling that whatever they faced, they needed each other's help. "It isn't enough, just to watch the rest of us struggle. Yeah, we're grateful that you pull people out of bad situations sometimes. But *sometimes* isn't good enough."

The Levitator shrank away from the rebuke. "Honestly, I don't know what more you want from me."

Philip cleared his throat. "Well, to start, *if* we're able to bring the song back to Earth, we'll need help spreading it over the globe. I don't have any idea how to do that. Do you?"

When the Levitator didn't answer, Philip continued. "This is exactly the kind of thing the Society of Lighthouse Keepers is best at. They could help us."

"You want me to bring one of them here? I don't know. It's one thing to grab someone who's already moving through the portal and redirect them. But to snatch an unsuspecting person who's not even involved in this conflict—"

"No one is uninvolved," Katherine interrupted. "Not anymore."

The Levitator winced. He played with the strands of spider silk at his elbow. "I'll think about it. And while I do, there's one more thing you need to take care of before you leave."

"What do you mean?" Griffin scowled. He was done trusting this kid.

"You'll be able to speak with the Marisians when you meet them—the portal will prepare you just as it did when you journeyed here. But there is one more protection Caligo can offer, and you would be unwise to leave for Maris without it."

The Levitator tipped back his head to speak with his attendant. Leónie answered in a terse whisper and a hushed argument began. At length, Leónie pivoted to acknowledge the Fenn family, a sour twist pulling at her mouth. She extended her arm toward the open air, where a pair of boats bobbed, waiting. "Follow me."

Griffin and his parents exchanged a worried look. Like most things where the Levitator was concerned, it didn't seem like they had any choice.

GRIFFIN

THE BOATS SPED down the currents of mist toward a squat building beside the markets. When the Fenn family stepped out onto the grated floor, they were greeted by whirring machines and a persistent dripping sound.

Leónie strode through a pointed arch that led into a bright room, sterile as a laboratory. One wall was lined with shelves holding hundreds of tiny glass jars. Another displayed racks of the filmy clothes all the Caligions wore. The third was scattered with standing desks bearing an assortment of funnels, bubbling vats, and curlicue tubing. And the far wall was covered, floor to vaulted ceiling, in iridescent webbing.

Hundreds of spiders hung from the webs, their

bodies shimmering in and out of sight. Some were as small as thumbtacks; others were as long and lanky as frogs. Griffin swallowed—or at least, he tried to. He wasn't scared of the daddy longlegs that lived in the garden, or the house spiders hiding in the corners of the old cottage. But these weren't anything like spiders from home. They watched the Fenns approach, their fangs clicking at odds with the hollow drip, drip, dripping from the distillery.

Leónie walked straight up to the wall of webs and bowed, her torso dipping so low her nose nearly brushed the grated floor. She straightened with a sniff and a little shake of her head and crossed to the racks of clothing. She picked three sets and handed one to each of the Fenns. Then she swiveled sharply and proclaimed: "It is the crypsis spider's choice to gift the people of Caligo with its magnificent excretions. We receive this gift every morning at sunrise."

Philip turned a little green. "Excretions?"

"What—did you think one would spit at you and you'd magically receive its powers of camouflage? The Levitator, in his infinite wisdom, has decreed that you three shall be endowed with the blessed crypsis juice."

"Endowed?" Griffin whispered. He didn't like the sound of that.

"The crypsis juice is our birthright. You three"—
Leónie looked down her nose at the Fenns—"were
certainly not born to this world. But it is the Levitator's wish, so far be it from me to—"

"We don't have time for this," Philip interrupted.
"What does it *do*?"

"*Do?*" Leónie's face bloomed an alarming shade
of purple. "The blessed crypsis juice doesn't *do* anything. It is a gift that you are spectacularly fortunate
to receive."

"And once we have received this . . . gift, then
what?" A hint of irritation crept into Katherine's
voice.

Leónie cleared her throat. Her skin rippled, shifting, and then she was gone. Griffin blinked. He
squinted at the spot where she'd been. Leónie was
still there—he could hear her indignant sniffing, but
the air where he *knew* she was standing had gone
hazy, blurred at the edges.

Katherine smacked her palm against her forehead. "Of course. If we travel to Maris looking like
this, the soldiers will spot us right away. And we
can't double the capacity of our lungs or grow a layer
of blubber like the Marisians have. We'll need to hide
in plain sight."

"And *that* will help us?" Philip bent at the waist

until he was eye level with the small jars. Each was filled three-quarters full with a silvery liquid, like watered-down mercury.

Katherine examined the silk garment draped over her arm. "This too, I'm guessing?"

Griffin sidled one step closer to the wall of spiders. "So how does it work?"

"*Work?*" Leónie sputtered as her skin rippled back to its usual coloring. "The blessed crypsis juice does not—"

"Oh, for Pete's sake. We drink it, right?" Philip reached out, uncapped three vials, and handed one to Griffin and another to Katherine.

"Right," Leónie said through gritted teeth. "Though you will not be able to shift in and out of view, as we can."

"But we'll blend in with whatever is behind us?" Griffin was still skeptical. "We'd be invisible?"

"That is correct, though it will be several hours before the crypsis juice takes effect. And it isn't some magic potion. It won't last forever."

Katherine raised her jar high, clinking it against Griffin's and Philip's. "Then there's no time to lose. To Maris!"

"To Maris," they echoed.

Griffin lifted the jar to his lips. He clamped his

eyes shut and pinched his nose. He tried to swallow as fast as he could, but that only made him sputter and choke instead. Philip pounded his back while Griffin coughed. The coughing turned to laughter, and soon all three Fenns were doubled over, holding tight to one another, for a moment leaving all their fears and uncertainty behind.

After a time, Katherine wiped her eyes and linked arms with Philip and Griffin. She tugged them upright, then dipped her head toward the Levitator's attendant and the wall of watching spiders. "Thank you for this gift. We will use it well."

GRIFFIN

THE FENN FAMILY had every intention of going straight to the lighthouse, but the boat stubbornly ferried them to the aerie where the Levitator waited, shifting his weight first to one foot, then the other, like a child who's been scolded.

As the boat neared the platform, he called out, "I did what you asked."

The Fenns looked from one to the other, perplexed. Griffin rubbed the backs of his hands against his eyes. Why did the Levitator have to be so mysterious all the time? Couldn't he ever just come out and say anything?

Philip froze, half in, half out of the boat. "Wait—you mean the Keepers? You made contact?"

"Even better." The Levitator swept his arm toward the aerie. "Follow me."

Griffin hurried to catch up, only to slam into his dad's back when he rounded the corner. He peered around Philip's shoulder. An elderly woman with deep lines carved into the skin beside her mouth stood alone, gripping her own elbows as if she were struggling to hold herself together. Her braids were white as the mists that enveloped her, ending in tufts that curled up to tickle her earlobes. She was dressed in a pilled sweater and baggy corduroys tucked into a pair of worn boots.

"Beatrix?" Griffin cried.

"You!" She unfolded her arms and pointed right at him. More lines crisscrossed her forehead. "You nicked my stola. I got in big trouble for that."

Griffin rushed forward to grasp Beatrix's hand in both of his. "I'm sorry—I never meant for you to take the blame. You were so nice to me. But I had to get my dad back, and none of the Keepers would listen to me. Good thing I did go, otherwise maybe we never would have realized . . ."

Beatrix gasped, her mouth dropping open. Her eyes were fixed on something, or rather someone, behind Griffin.

"Katherine?" Beatrix breathed. "Am I dreaming?"

Griffin's mom stepped forward and wrapped her arms around the older woman. "Thank you for taking care of my boy when he was all alone."

The frustration Griffin had felt toward the Levitator fizzled and burned out completely. He probably had no idea which one of the Keepers he'd dragged through the portal, and yet Beatrix was exactly who the Fenns needed. It wasn't only that the way her brain worked lined up with the sort of help they needed—it was more than that. When his dad disappeared and Griffin found himself thrust into the care of the Society of Lighthouse Keepers, it had seemed like he was surrounded by problems he couldn't solve and people he couldn't trust. Except for her.

And what they needed right now was someone they could trust.

"How did you get here?" Katherine asked.

"Talk to him." Beatrix nodded emphatically in the Levitator's direction.

"Yes, well . . ." Philip steered the tiny woman to a bench against the wall. "That may have been my doing. I didn't expect that he would—*ahem*. I suppose it's just as well. You see, Bea, we need your help."

Melanie Crowder

"Me?"

"Yes." Katherine settled on Beatrix's other side. "You."

"Shall I have some refreshments sent along?" the Levitator asked as he backed toward the door.

Griffin scrunched his nose and tried to shake his head so Beatrix would catch his meaning without the Caligions seeing and taking offense, but she only nodded absently. The moment the Levitator was gone, she whispered, "Who *is* that? Really—being yanked between worlds without a please or thank you—and by a child, no less!"

Philip chuckled. "They're a little pushy around here. We'll fill you in later, I promise."

"But we don't have time now," Katherine said.

"Right." Beatrix rolled her neck, then blinked several times to gather her wits about her. "What can I do?"

"The priests have been to Earth—you must know this."

"Of course. Not that the Keepers have done anything about it. With Dr. Hibbert locked inside her glass office, and guards watching her every move, we're split down the middle. Half want to give up and hand everything over to the Coast Guard, while the other half are tripping over one another trying to figure out how to shut the portal down for good."

"You've all got the malva vine protecting you, at least?"

"Oh, those priests won't get inside *my* head. But none of us are trained to fight. Once we discovered the priests were after trained soldiers whom they could control, the Keepers had to retreat. We went to the Coast Guard in the end anyway. They set patrols at the portal day and night, but the damage is already done, I'm afraid."

"But the patrols don't have any malva vine— what's stopping the priests from taking them, too?"

"If you can believe it, the Coasties stuff their ears full of cotton and wear helicopter headsets so they can't hear a thing the priests say."

Griffin blanched. That was it? Earplugs and some headphones? That was the best Earth could do?

Beatrix continued, "The rest of the armed forces are on alert now too. If the priests come back for more soldiers, it won't be so easy."

"But they will be back." Katherine sat forward, propping her elbows on her knees. "Beatrix, we think the ocean's song on Maris might be able to shield everyone on Earth from the priests' magic."

Beatrix tapped her fingers slowly in time with

her thoughts. "Clever. You believe it will behave the same way in our ocean?"

"That's the idea. But millions of people are land-locked, too far away to hear the ocean. We need somehow to disperse the song inland."

"We're leaving for Maris any minute. The Levitator, as you've discovered by now, can pull people from one world into another if they stand near enough to the portal. If we're successful, and we collect the song from Maris—"

"When."

"*When* we collect the song, he'll pull us through, from Maris straight to Earth."

"And if you stay in our cottage, the alarm will sound when we arrive," Griffin added.

"We'll get the song into the water somehow. But we need a way to spread it inland. Can you help?"

Beatrix's eyes darted side to side as if she were scanning a newspaper. "I don't know *how* yet, but yes, I'll find a way."

The Fenns reached out and drew her into a hug. "We have to go. With any luck, we'll see you again very soon."

Beatrix stepped away, shooing them toward the door. "I'll be ready."

FI

FI LANDED ON her feet in the lantern room. She shook her head to clear it, the smell of smoke heavy in her nostrils. Beside her, and scattered along the stairs below, the greenwitches were collapsed, keening gut-wrenching cries of anguish. Fi blinked, confused, and twisted to look out the bank of windows behind her.

Fire. The wildlands were on fire. The ground all around the tower was black, littered with charred tree stumps. To her left was all that remained of the green. To her right, scorched soil led to a flickering wall of orange and black columns of smoke rising into the sky. The boundary between the ground held by the soldiers and the resistance was fire.

"Up!" Fi doubled over, coughing. "Get up!"

She hooked her arms under Ness's armpits and pulled. Ness gritted her teeth and hauled herself to her feet. Together, they charged down the stairs, half-blinded by the smoke stinging their eyes.

The air cleared a little when they reached the ground floor and Fi swayed on her feet, drawing breath deep into her lungs. She closed her eyes, searching for the green. It sputtered, then flared to life against her eyelids. What should have been a tangle of green pulsing through the entire world was a spotty map of all that was left. Drips of flame seared the veins of trees that had stood for centuries, and ripped through fragile blossoms.

Fi gasped. It felt like someone had reached into her chest and squeezed. Hard. A headache stabbed the insides of her skull, and her skin singed and burned. She clung to the stair rail, struggling to stay on her feet. How long had it been like this? Were they too late?

Val braced herself against the workroom window. "Start with the roots." She gasped between words, pain written over her face. "The trees would want us to use their last bits of life, if it might save the rest."

The greenwitches nodded. They staggered toward the door leading out of the tower, leaning on one another for strength. They threw it open, expecting to fight their way out of the fort the soldiers had erected when Somni first invaded. But it was gone. The fort had stood for a hundred years, blocking access to the portal. Now holes had been hacked into the exterior wall of pikes and the gate was missing completely. Black rectangles in the dirt were the only sign that the barracks, jail, and mess hall had ever even been there. A thrill shivered through Fi. The resistance had done this. They were finally fighting back!

The greenwitches split in half. Val gathered one group around her and they charged directly toward the fire. Ness dragged Fi to catch up with the second group retreating into the wildlands. As Fi ran, the smell of smoke ebbed and her headache receded. The trees reached out to cover her like a cool cloth across her brow.

Suddenly voices filled her head and the ground beneath her began to ripple. She glanced over her shoulder. The tremor was coming from Val and the other greenwitches advancing on the fire. Their pleas were like something out of a dream, nipping at the edges of her mind.

Long-buried roots tore out of the soil, shaking dirt into the sky and snaking through the air like whips. The roots began to beat at the ground, stamping the flames into sparks. More churned above the surface, turning over the soil and smothering the sparks where they smoldered.

"Fi! Don't waste the cover they're giving us." Ness pointed to the top of the barren hill on the other side of the fort. "Look."

A line of red-robed priests marked the green-witches' advance. Soldiers filed in behind them, weapons at the ready. Fi skidded to a stop. There were only six greenwitches—what could they do against so many soldiers? Ness yanked Fi's collar, dragging her toward the trees, the air cooling as the canopy covered them. "Leave it. They know what they're doing."

Fi slipped in the thick undergrowth, falling hard to the ground. "We waited too long. We should have been here all this time. I have to help them!"

"Fionna," Ness pleaded, "Eb wasn't the only one who gave his life to get you here. Are you going to throw away that gift now? To do what—to sacrifice yourself?"

Fi struggled against Ness's grip and the green-witch abruptly released her. Ness dropped onto her knees, spreading her fingers wide and thrusting them into the soil.

"How do you know about Eb?" Fi's voice trembled. She scrambled to her feet.

"I told you we were in communication with the resistance. When they learned of our plans for you, they warned me how stubborn you can be."

"They?" Fi backed slowly away, then turned to run in the opposite direction.

Ness grimaced. "I didn't want to have to do this."

Before Fi had taken three steps, a cloying odor rose above the smoke and ash. It seeped into her lungs, slowing her mind. Fi stumbled. Her legs buckled, her arms suddenly heavy as tree trunks, and she crumpled to the ground.

15

FI

WHEN FI CAME to, everything was rocking, her head bobbing on her neck like a poppy at the end of a long stem. She tried to blink, but her eyelids were heavy as rain-soaked logs. Bogbean dotted the soil below and ivy climbed, unrestrained, over tree trunks and along the branches. When she twisted her neck, squinting against the glare, the sky swung overhead where it belonged. A moan escaped her lips and the rocking stopped.

She was settled gently onto the ground, but the "gently" part did nothing to improve the fact that she'd been slung across someone's shoulder like a bundle of sticks. If her eyes would only focus and her head stop spinning, she'd let Ness have it. How *dare* she? That wasn't what the green magic was supposed to be used for, even if they were at war, even if they were changing the rules as they went.

Fi squeezed her eyes shut and tried one more time to look around her. More than fifty people stared down at her, resistance fighters filling in the spaces between trees. They weren't half-starved, like the Vineans on Somni. They were strong, and ready to fight.

Fi gulped back her joy at the sight and swayed to her feet. "I can walk." Her voice was thick from disuse. How long had she slept?

Ness appeared in front of her, a somber twist to her lips. "Walk, then. We have a long way to go until we can stop for the night."

Fi scowled, swatting away the arm Ness offered. "I don't need your help."

"Suit yourself."

Fi took a few lurching steps forward before whirling back around. "You had no right to control me like that. I make my own decisions. I've earned that much."

"Fionna, I did what I had to do."

"Oh yeah?" Fi teetered closer, until she was nose-to-nose with the greenwitch, no longer caring that everyone watched her struggle to stay on her feet. "What makes you think you're one bit better than those priests? That's *exactly* the kind of thing they'd do."

Ness recoiled and Fi turned her back on the green-witch. She'd crawl through the wildlands before she took help from *her*. Fi focused on putting one foot in front of the other. Nobody was going to sling her over their shoulder again, not if it took every last bit of strength she had to keep herself upright.

Instead of marching in a line, the resistance fighters spread themselves thin. Leaves ducked away from their footfalls and the groundcover sprang back after each step. If the soldiers came looking, they wouldn't find a single trail leading to the outpost deep in the wildlands.

They walked for hours before Ness tried again, this time with a handful of snacks and some water as a peace offering. "I am sorry," she said. "I had no right to do that. Much as being on Somni changed you, living for decades on Caligo changed me too. It's no excuse, but I haven't often been confronted with something like, well, you."

Fi accepted the food and water grudgingly. "What happened back at the fort, anyway? Are the green-witches okay?"

"We couldn't stay to find out. They'll meet up with us as soon as they're able." Ness tried a smile.

"Don't underestimate them. They have been waiting a long time for this."

Fi coughed into her fist, the smoke still working its way out of her lungs. "Where are we going?"

"To the resistance outpost, deep in the wildlands."

Of course. Fi had never been to the outpost. Most of her childhood had been spent in hiding with Aunt Ada. And the Vineans she'd lived with on Somni—Liv and Eb—they'd never talked about it. Then again, they hadn't talked about much from home. It was easier being stuck on Somni if you didn't think too hard about what you'd left behind.

They walked until the sun dropped below the canopy, until there was nothing to show the way except moonlight glinting off waxy ribwort leaves. They walked until the thickets and meadows and jungle vines all blended together. They forded lime-green rivers, the water reaching up to Fi's ribs, unseen aquatic plants snaking aside to let them pass. They walked until the sky behind them began to gleam a pale gold. They walked until Fi was sure she'd collapse again, this time from exhaustion.

All through the long journey, Fi could feel the fiery edge of the wildlands just out of reach, the boundary between the scorched land held by the soldiers and the last of the green. It stretched from the fort into the very heart of Vinea, a constant reminder of how close the invaders were.

Fi let her eyes drift closed and the green rose up, in beads of pure life coursing through the plants all around her. It seemed to all flow in one steady direction, leading the way forward. Without opening her eyes, she continued forward, more sure of her footing than she had been before. Fi lost track of the hours, and the people all around her, and the reason for the long journey.

And then, seemingly out of nowhere, "Fionna?"

Her eyes snapped open. Fi stopped so suddenly she nearly toppled over. A woman stood at the edge of a secluded glade, her face in shadow. Fi gasped. Was she dreaming? Had she fallen asleep standing up?

"Aunt Ada?"

Her aunt was just as Fi remembered her, and yet not. The grief had worn away, and hard lines had taken its place. Her yellow hair was trimmed blunt beneath her earlobes. And she carried herself differently—not the hunched, frail frame of someone in hiding, but the bowstrung strength of a person who has taught her body to fight back.

Fi ran across the glade and flung herself into her aunt's arms. Her breath wavered, her throat closing over anything she might have said. She dropped her head against Ada's shoulder, the struggle to keep herself upright all through the long night draining out of her.

Ada released her grip, tucking the ragged ends of Fi's hair behind her ears. "We've been waiting and *waiting* for you to come home." She cinched her arm around Fi's ribs, drawing her deeper into the wood. "You must be exhausted."

The others fell back as Ada led Fi toward a wall of rust-colored brush. Towering trees rose from foliage so thick it seemed impassible. Fi ducked under a curtain of dripping moss, then scrambled over a rotting log. When she slid over the other side, the ground dropped off abruptly. Fi stumbled away from the edge, pinwheeling her arms to regain her balance. Vines stretched across the top of a broad hollow, masking its true floor beneath. She couldn't see a single person down there, not with her eyes open. But when she closed them, the green revealed false walls and temporary roofs hiding the resistance members below. It was the outpost, hidden in plain sight.

They descended ledges cut into the dirt, following the slope gradually downward. The ceiling of broad-leafed lichens and fern fronds let the sunlight through in spears that struck the cavern floor like spotlights. When they reached the ground, Ada led

Fi and the others to a narrow room with a long table stretching through its center.

"Sit and eat. Let me try to answer what I'm sure are a million questions shaking loose in that head of yours." Ada sat beside Fi, one arm around her waist, the other reaching to draw platters and pitchers close. She waited until Fi had begun to eat before continuing.

"There are things I could have told you before you left for Somni, things maybe I should have. The truth is, I thought you'd be safer if you didn't know all of it." Shadows played over Aunt Ada's face, deepening the wrinkles around her eyes and along the flat planes of her cheeks. "You should begin to feel it soon."

"Feel what?"

Aunt Ada sent a reproachful look over her shoulder in Ness's direction.

"We didn't have time—we had to cut her training short."

Ada nodded. "Fionna, a greenwitch can learn to see the green before her at all times, to feel it thrumming through her veins, and to hear it as clearly as you hear me speaking now. You learned a little about this on Caligo?"

"Yes."

"But here, on Vinea, the green will come looking

for you, too. It chooses how strong your power will be, and how it will move through you. Any training you may have been given on that other world was only so you would know how it feels when the power rushes into you—so it wouldn't paralyze you the first time it happened."

Fi frowned. "You think the green will come looking for me?"

"We do. One greenwitch serves as the direct conduit between us and the green. Your great-aunt Una was the last chosen. Before she died, she was given a vision of the one who would come next, the one who could save us all when things looked darkest." Ada interlaced her fingers over one knee and leaned back. "It was you she saw, Fi."

A buzz like a cloud of insects swarmed Fi's head. "But I barely know what I'm doing. And my veins don't even glow right."

Ada offered a small smile while she waited for the next volley of questions from her niece.

"I don't understand why you sent me away. If I'd stayed on Vinea, and trained as a greenwitch should, maybe I'd be ready now to fight—maybe I'd be strong enough to really help."

Aunt Ada ticked her head to the side. "There were some who didn't want you to go. But it would have been very dangerous to stay." She nibbled at her lower lip. "And anyway, Una was adamant that in order for you to come into your strength, you had to leave."

The resistance fighters and the other green-witches had settled into seats at the long table, but they hadn't begun eating, despite the long day of travel. Each one watched Fi, like they were waiting for miracles to sprout from the roots of her hair or something. Fi dropped her gaze to her lap. She was learning to see the green, and to work with it a little at least. But all that hope on their faces? It was too much. It curdled her stomach like nut milk left out on a warm day.

She was an excellent spy, and she wasn't afraid to say so. She was a fighter. She was brave. But magic? Somehow she was supposed to singlehandedly save them all? Fi cringed away from their stares. Impossible. They had the wrong girl.

16

FI

AFTER A HOT bath and a nap that stretched well into the afternoon, Ada led Fi beyond the outpost to the edge of the wildlands. When Liv saw Fi stroll up with the greenwitches, she gave a short, sharp laugh and clapped her arms around her former charge, lifting her off the ground. She set Fi down again with a grunt and a smile.

"It's good to see you, girl."

Back on Somni, Liv was always watching Fi like a hawk, handing out orders and monitoring how closely her instructions were followed. Until they stormed the temple, Fi hadn't known for sure that Liv was a leader in the resistance, though she'd wondered. It was one thing to observe the cunning behind Liv's directives, but it was another thing entirely to see her surrounded by her commanders and issuing orders like a general.

Eb had known about the magic dormant inside her, Fi was sure of it. Had Liv known, too? In all that time, she hadn't dropped a single hint. Fi's chin began to tremble and she bit down hard. Liv was just being Liv. Doing exactly what was needed to get the resistance to the point where they could fight back. It wasn't a betrayal, not really.

So why did Fi suddenly feel so alone?

She leaned forward, listening while Liv explained to the greenwitches how the soldiers from Earth wore goggles that helped them see like cats at night. It was how they'd so quickly identified the children with magic inside them. They also had long-range weapons that could fire across the barren lands, so an all-out charge was pointless. The resistance had been backpedaling, struggling to adapt to this new enemy. Before the greenwitches' arrival, they had begun preparing to retreat.

But now, finally, the resistance had a surprise of its own. The commanders were scrambling to adjust plans and shift fighters. They were pouring everything into the upcoming battle, knowing that if things didn't go their way, it would be their last.

The greenwitches left the fighters to their strategy,

making for the copse of trees at the top of the hill that marked the edge of the wildlands. Ness beckoned, but Fi hesitated, torn. She still felt like she belonged here, with Liv and the resistance. Maybe someday she'd believe her place was with the greenwitches, but she didn't, not yet.

She turned away from Liv, reluctantly following Ness up the hill. When Fi reached the top, she braced herself against the trees and stared out across the smoking soil. Ash drifted off the leaves above, settling in her hair like snow. The soldiers had made a hasty camp, placing a ring of tree trunks shaved to points around the perimeter and setting them deep into the ground.

The children were trapped inside that camp, likely terrified. Fi could have been one of them, easily. She probably knew some of the girls from her time on Somni. She must have passed them in the rectory, or scrubbed the temple bricks side by side, never knowing that like her, they'd be greenwitches someday.

"Open yourself to the green," Ness said, and Fi jerked her attention back to the circle. "Listen for any answer it might send you. The resistance is ready, either for an attack or a retreat. They're waiting for us to tell them the shape this fight will take."

"But Val and the others aren't back yet. Shouldn't

we wait until all the greenwitches can join together?"

"Fionna, at some point you're going to have to trust yourself, and the great potential within you."

"Ness, I can't—"

"Try."

Patience had never come easily to Fi. But she closed her eyes anyway. She tried to listen. She did her best to focus, to shed her frustration, and surrender to whatever would be.

It didn't work.

When her eyes snapped back open, Ness sighed. "The tunnels, then."

All around, the greenwitches roused themselves from their meditation, their eyelids dragging upward, blinking reluctantly. They looked from one to the other, their faces grim.

"What?" Fi asked. "What tunnels?"

"It's the best plan we have, without guidance from the green. The scorched trees left craters where their roots used to be. Remember, I told you—all we need is one root hanging on to life. We can work with that. So Earth's soldiers can see in the dark. Can they see underground, too? We'll beat them there.

"On its own, the green can't rise up and free itself from the soldiers. It needs us for that. And we need it. We'll follow the green from root system to root system, tunneling beneath that camp, and we will take our children back."

"But won't the soldiers hear the ground moving? Won't they guess what we're trying to do?"

Ness dug her hands into the soil, turning her palms over and letting the dirt spill through her fingers. Fi had never seen her look so unsure of anything. "It's our best option. We can't wait any longer. We have to strike now, before the resistance is weakened any further."

Fi glanced around the circle. No one argued with Ness's words. No one offered another option. Instead, they stood and descended the hill to meet the resistance. Before Ness followed, she rested a hand on Fi's shoulder. "We have to trust in Una's vision that the green will choose you. Maybe it hasn't yet. But there's still time. And if it doesn't, if we're wrong, what choice do we have but to try to save this world ourselves the best we know how?"

Fi watched Ness trudge back down the hill. She hadn't felt this useless since that awful day when the soldiers attacked the cave where her family had been hiding. A sob broke from her lips. There had to be something she could do. She wasn't a little kid anymore. She couldn't still be that helpless.

Liv. Fi had earned her respect back on Somni. Liv

would listen. Fi stumbled down the hill, her tunic flapping behind her. "Liv!" she called. When she drew close, she whispered, "You didn't let them talk you in to that tunneling idea—"

Liv clapped Fi on the shoulder without breaking her stride. "It's already done."

"But we'll never get through the soldiers' defenses! They'll know we're coming once the ground begins moving beneath them."

"Fi." Liv fixed her with a stern look. "I know that the greenwitches' belief in you isn't an easy thing to shoulder. But you have a job to do. And you've always come through for me when I've given you an order, no matter how tricky. This is no different." With that, Liv strode away to pass word to the rest of her commanders.

Fi balled her hands into fists. This *was* different. She'd do anything for the resistance, anything within her power. It was easy enough when she was a spy— all she needed was to be brave, and a little sneaky. But magic? She couldn't *make* that happen. If the green didn't choose her, there was nothing she could do to change that.

There had to be another way. "Aunt Ada!" Fi dashed to her side. "You have to stop them, *please*. I'm not ready. I can't do what they say."

But it was already too late. The greenwitches separated, one to the head of each column of attackers waiting at the edge of the wildlands. Their voices filled her head, all talking over one another as they began the attack. Fi's eyes drifted closed and a groan slid past her lips. Magic swelled in the greenwitches all around her, so strong that she staggered back. Her aunt's arms closed around her waist, holding her up. The green pulsed at the edges of Fi's vision, flowing in a steady stream beneath the ground.

The greenwitches called to the dying trees, snags smoldering in the burned wastelands. With their last bit of life, the trees shifted their roots beneath the soil, tunneling toward the fort. A hole opened in the ground in front of the resistance fighters, dirt spilling like lava out of an eruption. The hole widened, musty air coughing out of the newly formed tunnel entrance. The fighters hesitated, and then they charged into the darkness. Behind Fi, still more fighters shouldered slingshots loaded with explosive sap, covering a third group that charged straight at the gate to distract the soldiers from the rumbling beneath the ground.

Ada sank to her knees, still cradling her niece, as the green rushed into Fi. It was supposed to be bliss, but all she felt was pain. The searing, singeing, terrible last gasp of life. It consumed her, but no lash of power flowed out of her fingertips. All she could do was watch helplessly as the Vinean assault broke on the soldier's camp.

"The second those kids are safe in the tunnels, light that place up," Liv shouted.

But they never got the chance.

Soldiers sprinted outside the fort, leveling their weapons at the rippling soil, each one pushing a Vinean child in front of him. The column of fighters advancing on the camp halted. They couldn't attack the soldiers without killing the children.

The next thing Fi knew, she was thrown backward through the air. A percussive blast hit her ears and the dirt fell away, dropping a trench in the ground. A cloud of dust rose to fill the sky. The tunnel collapsed and the life that had flowed underground—all those resistance fighters—just blinked out.

Fi screamed. She crawled onto her stomach. Everyone was staring at her—Ness, Liv, the fighters letting their weapons fall to the ground—their faces covered in a mix of confusion, grief, and betrayal.

They'd all believed she would save them, somehow, in the end. They were wrong.

GRIFFIN

THE FENN FAMILY lined up in front of the bull's-eye leading to Maris. All three wore the spider silk clothing Leónie had given them. Griffin tugged at the ends—it clung a little embarrassingly tight to the skin, and the trailing edges were ridiculous. They were only going to get in the way. But he had to admit, once you got past the whole *spider* part, it was softer even than the fancy sweater his grandparents had given him for his birthday last year, and not half as cold as he'd thought it would be.

The Levitator stood to one side of the lens, absently stroking the fuzzy thorax of a silver spider whose long legs wrapped around his arm. He looked nervous. He'd been smug plenty of times, or so unhurried it was infuriating. But nervous? That was new.

Griffin glowered. "What aren't you telling us?"

The Levitator seemed startled by the question. He dropped his hands to his lap. "All I can do is watch the fleet to make sure there are no holes in the net that holds up our city. I look into the portals, listen when I can, and pull people through if they get close enough. But that's about as far as my abilities go."

He paused, and there it was again—unease floating beneath his usual calm exterior. "There were good reasons why the old Levitator refused to interfere with other worlds. The truth is, I don't know what I'm sending you into."

Katherine put her shoulders back. "For all we know, everything we're doing could only make things worse in the end. But to *not* act in moments like this? Impossible. We can only do the best we know how. And hope." She looked into the faces of her husband and son. "Never lose hope."

"Are you sure? Wouldn't it be safer if one of you went while the others—"

"We stay together." Griffin gripped his mom's hand on one side and his dad's on the other.

The Levitator nodded, his fingers worrying the frayed end of his sleeve. He hesitated, then stepped away from the lens. "I'll be watching for you. If you need me, I'll be ready to yank you back here."

The tower walls began to shake. The glass bull's-eye sagged and started to spin. Griffin squeezed his eyes shut and gritted his teeth. The portal tugged at him, like it would suck his guts through his skin, and then it pulled him all the way through.

Griffin's legs buckled and he tumbled to the lantern room floor. Before he could lift his head to look outside and get his bearings, the whole place pitched to the left, and then to the right, tossing the Fenns around the room like laundry in a spin cycle. Philip grabbed the stairway railing as he careened past. He wrapped his legs around the metal and stretched his arms out to Griffin and Katherine.

"Grab on!"

They dragged themselves toward the stairs, fighting against the pitching ground, then slid down the steps, bellies to the floor.

"What is happening?" Griffin yelled.

"I don't know!" Philip called over his shoulder. "But it's better the farther down you get, I think."

The Fenn family slunk down flight after spiraling flight, until they reached the ground floor of the lighthouse. There, the rocking was more like swaying. Rhythmic, almost like waves.

"Hang on—" Griffin scrambled over to the

window. A huge wave broke against the tower with a *boom* that shook the foundation and rolled past, all the way to the horizon.

They were *on* the water. The lighthouse on Maris was a massive buoy.

Knowing what caused the tower to pitch like crazy side to side made room in Griffin's head for other things. Like the smell. It was different from the Oregon coast because, of course, there *was* no coast on Maris. No beached sea creatures spoiling in the sun. No mud flats filtering layers of detritus. Just the briny air, with none of the beach to go with it.

Another detail worked its way into Griffin's thoughts: The coast back home was full of birdsong—squawking and piping and chirping all day long. There was none of that here. But without any land to, well, *land* on, there wouldn't be, would there?

Instead of the birdsong, something else filled the air. It started out low, like waterlogged timbers groaning as they shifted. Then it altered, modulating higher and splitting into two distinct sounds. Griffin shivered. It wasn't just whale song, or the sound of wind whistling through the gallery railing above. It was the magic of this world. The song of the sea.

"Marvelous," Katherine whispered.

"At least no one's guarding the place." Philip

peered out the far window. "Anyone who ends up here would be stranded, I guess. We're floating in the middle of the ocean. Unless you have a boat, you're stuck."

In the lull between swells, Griffin staggered across the room to stand beside his parents. "Are *we* stranded, then?"

Philip nodded at the waves barreling past. "Well, there's no swimming that. We'll have to trust the old Levitator's notes."

Along the bricks surrounding them, tiny bones and broken shells were strung from looping lines. Griffin steadied himself against the brick wall and, just as the Levitator's notebook had instructed, combed through the dangling objects, searching for anything resembling a whistle.

"Found one," he announced, lifting it to his lips and blowing a long, sustained breath. He was pretty sure he'd done it right, but no sound came out.

"Me too." Katherine rose onto her tiptoes to reach a hollow bone, narrow and notched along one side. Her cheeks puffed and flattened as air moved through the whistle. Again, no sound. Philip found a third, but it, too, was silent.

Griffin peeked out the window, searching for any sign that their message had been received. The light was fading fast; only the revolving beams from the lens above illuminated the water below. The waves rolled past, the ocean's secrets hidden beneath dark swells.

Griffin slid down the brick wall. He drew his knees up to his chest and closed his eyes. It was a little like being on a ship, there at the base of the tower, rocking back and forth, back and forth, until the motion seemed as natural as standing on solid ground. He'd been out on the open ocean in fishing boats a dozen times. The waves had never bothered him; he'd *liked* the thrill of the pitching boat. But there was something different about these waves—something eerie about knowing there was no harbor to come into, no home on the headland to return to when the trip was over.

But if the old Levitator was right, *someone* was out there. Someone would be coming for them.

GRIFFIN

GRIFFIN WOKE WITH a start. Goose bumps rippled over his arms and legs. Something was out there, just beyond the door. He held his breath, listening. His dad was snoring, of course. Waves slapped against the base of the tower, and the ocean's song rose and fell in its never-ending melody.

But *there*—that was something else.

It was a clicking, warbling sort of call. Whatever was making the sound, it wasn't human. Griffin shook his mom and dad awake. Philip rolled to his feet, eyes darting around the dark room. Katherine moved more slowly, cocking her head and listening. She lifted a finger to her lips, then pointed to the door. Philip swept Griffin behind him and the three crept along the wall. Katherine drew the door toward her and peered out into the darkness.

The song of the sea was louder with the door open, almost as if it were greeting them. Without any dust in the air, the moon was so white it gleamed silver, its peaks and craters startlingly clear. Moonlight shivered across the crests of the incoming waves, and it glimmered across the backs of *something*—many large somethings—in the water beyond the buoy.

"Look!" Griffin whispered.

"Incredible," Philip murmured.

The moment they stepped out from the doorway, they were greeted by that same clicking, chirruping sound. It was *definitely* coming from those creatures. Their broad backs broke the water, revealing hornlike lobes to either side of gaping holes that could only be their mouths.

"Are they some kind of ray?" Philip whispered.

"Gigantic manta rays, maybe."

"So they're not dangerous, then?" Griffin swallowed.

"I wouldn't say that."

"They certainly seem to want something from us."

"I think . . ." Griffin couldn't believe what he was about to say. "I think they want us to come with them."

At that, the giant rays broke the surface in unison, the clicking rising in a crescendo.

A tentative smile crept over Katherine's lips. "I believe you're right."

She exchanged a look with Philip, the kind parents are always trading over their children's heads. Another kid might have minded. But that sort of thing was new for Griffin—the everyday kind of thing he never thought he'd have again—both parents fussing over him.

Philip raised an eyebrow. "If we do nothing, Somni will control everyone on Earth. And they'll use our armies to attack the other worlds."

"If we do nothing, we'll have no home to return to," Katherine added. "Nowhere will be safe."

So they stepped together to the edge of the lighthouse buoy. The air was calm, and warm even though the sun had been down for hours. The buoy tipped toward the waves and then away from it, toward and away. Griffin eyed the staircase leading down. They were going to swim with those rays—that much was clear. But were they supposed to just walk into the waves?

Before he could move toward the stairs, the giant rays dipped into the water, disappearing from sight. Griffin peered over the edge, then jumped back as one of the rays leaped out of the water to his right, twisting in midair, its slick back brushing so close to Griffin's nose that his hair blew sideways across his face. The ray twisted again as it cleared the end of the buoy, slapping down on the face of the water before sinking below. As soon as the first landed, a second launched into the air.

Griffin backed up until he was pressed against the whitewashed tower bricks. "They want us to jump on their backs? No way."

Philip grimaced, stepping up to the edge. "I'll go first."

Griffin darted forward to give his dad a quick hug. When the next ray leaped into the air, Philip squared his shoulders, lifted his arms, and leaned forward as if he were free diving off the edge of a cliff. But before he could fall, the ray was beneath him, flattening Philip against its back and carrying him under the water.

"Dad!" Griffin shrieked. He ran to the edge of the buoy, staring at the place where the ray had disappeared beneath the waves. He strained against his mother's arms holding him back from the edge.

Out at sea, the ray broke the surface again, vaulting into the air. Philip got in one ecstatic whoop before the ray slapped down on the surface again.

This time, though, the massive creature didn't dive. Instead, it skimmed the waves, curving in a slow arc until it faced the buoy where Griffin and his mom waited. Philip pulled his knees under him and sat up so he could raise an arm over his head, beckoning the others to join him.

"He's okay," Katherine breathed.

"He's okay," Griffin echoed, bracing himself. He had to go next—no way would his mom get in that water without him. And they couldn't stay on the buoy forever. It was only a matter of time before the soldiers discovered them.

The water parted to his right. A pair of horns and a gaping mouth broke the surface, rising toward Griffin. He let out a tight breath. *Come on. You can do this.* Before he could change his mind, Griffin stepped to the edge, raised his arms just like his dad had done, and leaned out over the water.

Time seemed to slow. The creature's silvery skin filled his vision, then the ray slid along Griffin's arms until his hands hooked on the base of the wings. Griffin winced, half expecting his shoulders to be ripped out of their sockets, but instead, the giant ray twisted, balancing Griffin like a teacup on its broad back. He barely had to remember to hold on. The wings or fins or whatever they were stretched out to either side, lifting the kitelike body and thrusting it into the air.

Abruptly, the balance shifted and they weren't going up anymore; they were speeding down. Griffin squinted his eyes against the sting of the salt, and *smack!*—they hit the surface, sinking below, seawater spilling over the ray's sleek body and rushing for Griffin. He sucked in a breath and hung on with everything he had.

19

FI

FI STUMBLED AWAY from the failed battle, her eyelids stuck together in a paste of tears and ash. Blinded by anguish, she left the cover of the trees, stumbling into the tall grasses, the feathery tips brushing along her jaw and collarbone. The green pulsing through the wildlands coursed through her, beating back the taste of death and smoke and failure in her mouth.

Fi ran until she couldn't feel that pain anymore, past the meadow, through a bog that sucked at her ankles, and under the cover of an ancient stand of gnarled yew trees. She dragged the backs of her hands across her eyelids, smearing the grit until she could open her eyes again.

A shiver rippled through her as she stepped over some invisible marker on the land. Branches shifted overhead, bending to form the ribbed roof of a chapel. Fi spun in a slow circle as a steady rain began, splattering on the leaves and funneling into pools marking the oblong boundary of the chapel even as it formed, the drips pealing like bells as they landed.

She lifted her face to the sky, letting the rain beat against her skin, letting the ache inside her chest swell until she thought she might burst. Fi swatted at a line of raindrops. She wasn't the all-powerful greenwitch Vinea needed her to be. She didn't deserve this holy space.

Fi squeezed her eyes shut and she was back there, in the battle—the resistance fighters smothered underground. They died because she couldn't do what everyone thought she could.

She was only herself. Stubborn, impatient, all-too human Fi. How could she be any different? But Great-Aunt Una had believed she could be more. Was that why Eb had stepped in front of the blow meant for her—because there was supposed to be something special about Fi? Something she could do to save Vinea that no one else could?

Only, she hadn't. She couldn't.

Fi had run away from the battle, but she hadn't been able to outrun the hot breath of shame. She sagged against the sessil tree at the heart of the chapel. The lowest branches stretched well over her head, the highest ones whipping in the wind at the top of the canopy.

Fi swept the tears from her cheeks. She had to face this. She laid her palm against the gnarled trunk and the tree nudged back.

Up?

The lowest branch bent down to where she stood. As it reached for her, Fi wrapped her arms around the bark, swinging herself up to standing as she was lifted high above the ground. She held on, stunned at the raw power of the chapel that she'd been able to draw from. A second branch arced toward her, and then a third. She rose through the heights until the green was beneath her and all that was before her was sky.

From that height, Fi could barely make out the flashing beams from the lighthouse fighting to cut through thick clouds of smoke. Behind her stretched the wildlands, its borders shrinking by the minute. Beyond that, land burned black and riddled with snags. And in front of her, far too close to where the chapel stood, the soldiers' camp with the children trapped inside.

Fi's lungs ached. The silty air scraped her throat until it was raw and swollen. She couldn't bring herself to look away, not after everything that had gone so terribly wrong. Not after what she'd done. Or couldn't do.

She stayed in the crook of that highest branch so long that she lost track of the crimson sun sinking down, of the sturdy tree beneath her, of her own arms and legs, and the steady beating of her heart. Perhaps it was the smoke pouring into her lungs that eased her eyes closed, that beckoned her gently toward sleep.

While she slept, she dreamed. She was running frantically away from something. Every time she looked over her shoulder, the ground rose up like a mudslide, threatening to swallow her. The landscape before her flickered between the barren soil of Somni and the scorched wasteland of Vinea. She ran and she ran, but the avalanche of rocks and dirt and dead limbs never stopped coming.

Fi woke, groggy, on the forest floor. A dozen ferns covered her like a canopy bed, hiding her from sight in case anyone wandered by. The fronds parted as she sat up. Her fists clenched handfuls of soil. She swallowed, wincing, her throat hoarse from screaming. Slowly, her fingers uncurled. There in her palm was a seed, its shell firm and glinting dully.

The plants all around her lifted off the ground, straining against their roots. Leaves curled and fiddleheads unfurled, all reaching toward that single seed. Fi sat still as a stone. She hadn't done anything—she wouldn't even know how to ask them to do that. It must be the green trying to show her something. But what?

She brushed the soil away from the seed.

She barely breathed.

A memory crept out of the dark, flooding her mind. She could smell the sharp Somni air, taste the moisture wicking off her tongue. It was during her first month on that strange world, and she'd been running an errand for Eb on the outskirts of the city. For the first time, she'd witnessed the raze crews at work.

She'd nearly cried out, dropped everything and dashed over to them. She longed to shake the sleeves of their stolas, begging for anything they might have heard about her family who'd been taken. But the sight of the soldier standing guard at the end of the line of prisoners stopped her. In the end, she'd crouched behind a low wall and watched their slow passage.

At first glance, the raze crew seemed to be doing exactly what they were supposed to, seeking out life growing in the barren soil and ripping it out, roots and all. But as Fi peered closer, she realized that wasn't what was happening. Not exactly.

The prisoners worked with small pickaxes, slicing through the soil so they could tear the roots from the ground. But even as the right hand shook the dirt from one plant and set it into a sack strung over their shoulders, the left scattered seed into the broken ground. Yes, they were uprooting life, but they were sowing it, too. For every plant they killed, they let loose a dozen seeds.

Fi shook her head. The memory was still there—like a film over her mind, fading even as she reached for it. There was something different about those seeds. Something familiar. What *was* it?

Fi pressed her fingers to her temples. She knew what she'd seen. She knew the green had somehow called that particular memory into her mind. But what was she supposed to understand?

FI

FI SCRAMBLED THROUGH the underbrush, sprinting for the outpost. Strands of hair whipped like cobwebs across her face and ashes fell like rain, singeing everything they touched. She hurried past the sentries and down the steps cut into the wall of the hollow. Four greenwitches were gathered around the conference table, deep in conversation with Liv, Aunt Ada, and their commanders. Fi dashed inside, planted her hands on the tabletop, and announced, "I have to go back to Somni."

Ness stopped midsentence, her eyes hard as she turned on Fi. "That's ridiculous."

"No, I'm serious."

"After everything we went through to get you home? Fi, our fight is here."

Fi shook her head, struggling to catch her breath. "You thought it was *me* that was special. It's not, and you know it. I don't understand the green magic like you do. I can't do a fraction of the things Val can. And yeah, maybe someday I'll be as powerful as Great-Aunt Una. But I'm just a kid. I can't save everyone. I can't."

Fi gulped. She loved it already, the magic of her green world moving through her. She turned to her aunt, pleading. "You know me. If there's anything special about me, it's that I'm stubborn. I never gave up hope of coming back here. I never gave up on our family the soldiers captured. I still believe some of them are alive somewhere on the raze crews, waiting to return to us."

Liv stepped forward, laying a hand on Fi's shoulder. "You have to let that go."

"No." Fi shrugged off her hand. "We have to bring them back. *They* are the answer, not me. Or maybe, yeah, *me*—because I'm the only one who won't forget about them.

"Just listen. The raze crews have been sowing a net of seeds all over Somni. The seeds have been incubating, waiting for the right time to burst into life. Waiting to be *called*." Fi whirled on Ness. "Think about it—here on Vinea, there are seeds everywhere, even where all the green has been burned to the ground. I can list a hundred plants that only come to life after a fire, the ones that need heat to break open their hulls to let the first bit of green through."

Ness pursed her lips. "Greenwitches can't speak to a seed, Fi. I told you there are limits to what we can do. We need shoots and buds, vines and roots. We can't call the green into being. We can only work with what's already alive."

The more Fi spoke, the more certain she became. "*You* can't. But what if they can?"

Ada crossed her arms over her chest. "You think there are greenwitches on the raze crews? Impossible. Fi, the soldiers would kill them. The green awakening in their veins—the glow—it would give them away."

"Maybe. But maybe not. The green doesn't glow in me like it does in the rest of the greenwitches. It's dimmer, hardly there at all. Face it—something about being on Somni changed the way the magic works in me. But that doesn't have to be all bad, not if it helps us when nothing else can."

"Fionna, don't be foolish," Ness pleaded.

"What if you're wrong? What if it's not that

greenwitches have all the power and no one else has any? What if every Vinean has a pinch of the green magic in them? What if it's not about who's the most powerful, or about one person saving us all?" Fi took a deep breath. "I have to go. I have to find out."

"Absolutely not. We need to retreat, and we can't afford to waste time arguing. We have to face the fact that Somni has won."

Fi planted her hands on her hips and her feet in the soil, trying to sound braver than she felt. "I'm going back to Somni whether you believe me or not. What—are you going to spell me again? Go ahead. Try."

Aunt Ada crossed the ground between them and settled her arm over Fi's shoulders. "I'll go with you as far as the tower."

Relief sighed out of Fi's lungs. She wasn't completely alone, then.

Liv threw her hands in the air. "She's your problem now—but you should know that soldiers have been crawling all over the tower since the greenwitches came through. I can't spare a single fighter to protect your passage."

"I won't need it," Fi said, thrusting her chin out. "The green is with me." As she spoke, the ground beneath her shifted, broad leaves turning flat like a shield behind her, vines unwinding from their perches and twining around her slight form.

Liv quirked an eyebrow at the others. "You wanted a sign from the green? I think you just got it."

FI

AFTER SOLDIERS HAD raided the cave where their family lived, Ada and Fi were the only family the other had. They were terribly lonely and stricken by grief. In every shadow, Fi imagined soldiers waiting to snatch them. Each night, death lurked in her dreams. Within weeks, bold little Fi had been reduced to a frightened child.

And so Ada set her own fears aside, beating back monsters real and imagined, teaching her niece to stand and face the thing that terrified her, again and again, until she was master of her own mind. Soon both of them possessed a strength of will greater than Ada had imagined possible. They were everything to each other, their suffering and their survival binding them together every bit as much as their love.

Just as she had done so many times as a child, Fi reached out and took her aunt's hand and they walked alone through the wildlands. They traversed the undergrowth together, winding their way through shaded glades and over trickling streams.

Ada's jaw was set, but worry creased the skin around her eyes and pinched her lips together at the edges. Fi should have refused when her aunt offered to come. But they had been apart for two years already, and here she was, leaving again. She'd take whatever time they could get together.

The closer they drew to the edge of the wildlands, the more the air clouded, the more their long journey weighed on them both. A grim coating of ash smeared across the face of the leaves and dusted the soil. Each breath became strained. They stopped beneath the broad branches of an old sycamore and Fi sank to the ground, leaning against the solid trunk and letting it prop her up for a few breaths.

Ada settled beside her. "You know I want our family to be all right, to have survived the ambush all those years ago. But are you certain you want to do this?"

Fi tilted her head back, peering through the lattice of branches overhead. "I have to." She grimaced, searching for the right words. "I met this boy from

Earth named Griffin. When he first showed up on Somni, he did everything wrong—I thought he was going to bring the whole resistance down."

She shook her head. "But he was so sure that was exactly where he needed to be. He would have done anything to save his dad. And nothing I could say, or Liv, or Eb, or Arvid, or anyone else would stop him. It's like that. I can't explain why I'm so sure we need the raze crews. I just *know* it."

Aunt Ada dropped her head to the side until it rested against Fi's. "Sometimes it's easier to believe in someone other than ourselves. You believe in the raze crews. Okay. Well, I believe in you."

Fi tucked herself under her aunt's chin, wrapping her arms tight around her waist. "Thank you."

A forest is a symphony of sound, if you know how to listen. Trees groan and shift in their own time, petals rustle as they splay open, and pollen splatters every time it touches down. Fi and Ada listened with their whole beings, soaking in the little noises of the forest that had been their comfort in those early years.

Fi pulled away at last with a sigh. "I know my great-aunts and -uncles might not have made it, and even Aunt Gee or Aunt Nan. I *do* know that. But I have to try."

Ada stood, brushed the dirt from her leggings, and extended both arms to Fi. "Then we'd better get you there, quick as we can."

They crouched in the undergrowth, watching the tower for any sign of the soldiers Liv had warned would be on patrol. But there was no movement in the burned-out fort or the tower at its center.

"Are you sure you don't want to wait until dark?" Aunt Ada twisted her lips, her face creased with worry.

Fi let out a mirthless laugh. "They've got goggles for that, remember? No, I need to go now. Either the green will protect me, or it won't. Waiting won't change that."

Ada clasped her in a tight hug. "Be careful. Please."

"I will," Fi whispered.

Her aunt backed away as Fi crept forward, darting behind bits of rubble strewn around the remains of the fort before dashing forward again. She was halfway to the tower when she heard a twig snap behind her. Fi whirled around.

Four soldiers tracked her, the closest one a single step away. Each pointed a matte black weapon with a hollow snout straight at her. Fi froze. Ness had taught her what to say if she needed protection. It had only been a few days before. But in that moment, she couldn't call a single word to mind.

The soldiers closed rank, their eyes dull and their faces blank. Fi backed away from their advance, glancing around the rubble. The priest controlling them couldn't be far. Terror seized her, the same terror she'd lived with all that time on Somni, certain that a single misstep, a look, even, would mean the end for her.

Just then, a breeze rustled through the trees at the edge of the wildlands. It sent the smell of wet soil and newly opened buds and fresh blossoms wafting across her face. Her eyes drifted closed, and the green was there—at a distance, but close enough. It reached for Fi, burning away the fog in her mind. And she remembered.

Shield me?

The green answered with an audible *crack*, then a peculiar whistling sound. It took Fi a moment to place it, and when she did, her eyes grew wide. She bit down on her lip until she drew blood.

A healthy forest is home to all kinds of trees: saplings stretching skyward for a sliver of sunlight, young trees learning to withstand high winds and harsh droughts. And old growth, holding space in the canopy for the youngsters who will come after. When it's time for one of those giants to topple? It's a mighty thing to see.

Air whistled past the trunk and between the broad branches as the old tree shook the soil from its roots and crashed toward the ground. Fi watched it fall, watched the soldiers halt their advance and cock their heads, listening. Understanding dawned far too late.

Fi spun away, cringing away from the sound of splintering wood and breaking bones. She ran for the tower with everything she had.

GRIFFIN

GRIFFIN SHOULD HAVE been terrified. He was riding the backs of the biggest rays he'd ever seen, over the biggest waves he'd ever seen. Anything could be beneath the water—creatures with teeth as big as trees, or microscopic bugs that paralyze you if you swallow even one. Or sharks. Plain old sharks.

But as the giant ray rode the swells, calm settled over Griffin. The rays were protecting him and his parents, that much was clear. He didn't have any idea why, but much as his brain tried to come up with reasons he should be scared, he simply wasn't.

The trip was long, and after a time, the song of the sea and the rising and falling swells lulled him into a nodding near-sleep. The waves were black except where a glimmer of starlight caught the crests, and the stars winked above, muted by the dust of long-dead galaxies. Every so often, a flock of fish would break out of the water, soaring on the night winds before plunging down into the depths again.

The moon had set by the time the Fenns reached the docks suspended above the waves like a water skipper. Griffin had read about the aquaculture beds in the library back on Caligo, how the invading soldiers had forced the Marisians to cultivate a massive field of seaweed. They needed it to supply Somni with nutrients that that world could no longer produce on its own since, after the priests destroyed Somni's sjel trees and their dream clouds, hardly anything grew there anymore. After all, the priests needed to feed their army, even if they half-starved their own citizens.

The aquaculture beds were built like an upside down skyscraper. Towers of trellised seaweed reached deep into the water, their bulbous arms branching out and connecting the entire structure like steel triangles reinforcing a building. Bulbs lit from within bobbed and dipped with the current, dangling from every node.

On the surface, a series of docks stretched out from a central hub. Guard towers stood at the tip and bend of each dock, with the Marisians in the middle of it all, living beneath a sprawling roof they built to feel like the cabins of the boats they used to call home.

That's where the Fenns were headed: straight for the roof at the center of the docks. Griffin flexed and shook out his hands, trying to prepare himself for whatever they found up there. He startled, rubbing his fists into his eyes before shaking his hands again, directly in front of his face this time. Griffin nearly slid off the back of the giant ray in shock. He couldn't see his own hands. He could feel them, and the air where they should have been sort of wiggled. He looked down at his elbows, which flickered in and out of sight.

Griffin gasped. The crypsis juice—it was working!

He peered over his shoulder, and sure enough, his parents wavered in and out of view. How were they supposed to stay together if they couldn't even see one another?

The docks were balanced on sturdy pillars that allowed the waves to roll past with little to hinder their passage. When they drew near, the giant rays slowed their approach until they barely broke the water, their passengers flat on their backs, hidden under the cover of the cloudy predawn. Griffin's ray began treading water, pumping its fins against the current and raising its broad back to the height of the elevated docks.

Oh. Griffin swallowed hard. *We're supposed to jump.*

Griffin tucked his feet beneath him, crouching like a frog on the ray's broad back. When it followed the rolling wave to its highest point and lifted out of the water like a catamaran, Griffin sprang toward the docks. He bit down on a scream, pinwheeling his arms and legs as the planks reared up to meet him. Just when he thought he would crash, his parents caught him—his invisible parents. His mom's hand clamped over his mouth and his dad's arms steadied him.

The rays dipped beneath the waves one last time and were gone. Slowly, the Fenn family lowered themselves to the planks. The crypsis juice would camouflage them, but it couldn't disguise the sound of their footsteps or erase the wet marks they left behind. If the soldiers were looking closely enough, they'd spot the intruders.

So Griffin and his parents crawled across the dock, making for the thatched roof at the center that sheltered a web of hammocks stretched in overlapping spirals. As he drew closer, he could make out a central hearth, its smokestack venting through a wide hole in the roof's peak. Patterned mats blanketed the planks, littered with discarded children's toys and lumps of netting waiting to be mended.

Suddenly people tumbled out of the hammocks, lifting spears and sharp-tipped tridents at the Fenns' approach. A man and woman stepped out from under the roof's shadow, moonlight settling on circlets of glimmering shells over their temples.

"Who's there?"

Griffin froze. The voice was impossibly deep, and no wonder—that man's chest was huge. Griffin felt his mom pull away, and heard her deliberately cross the last few steps to meet the Marisians.

"Mom!" he whispered, reaching out to pull her back. But when his hands closed on air, he panicked. He couldn't see her. He couldn't feel her.

Philip's hand cupped the back of Griffin's neck, steady and calm. "This is what she does best."

The Marisian woman was every bit as tall as the man, her voice pitched only slightly higher. "Why can't we see you?"

"We've come from another world, from Earth," Katherine began. "Caligo's magic worker gifted us the ability to shift our skin to hide from Somni's soldiers, so we could meet with you." When they didn't respond, Katherine pleaded. "We need your help. Desperately."

Griffin and his dad rose to their feet, tiptoeing the last few steps until they stood shoulder to shoulder with Katherine. The Marisians squinted, seeming to barely trace their outlines. Katherine extended her hands, and the woman, wary but willing, reached out to grasp her forearms.

No one spoke, and so the rolling waves and the moaning docks and the beseeching song of the sea filled the air. Griffin watched the faces of the strangers all around him. They looked every bit as scared as he was. And a few seemed just as curious, too.

"We need your help. *Please*," Katherine urged. "We share the same enemy, and I'm convinced that we must join the magics of our worlds to defeat them. It's the only way."

The man glanced warily toward the nearest guard tower. "Come with us."

They stepped into the shadows beneath the thatched roof, and Griffin and his parents followed. They kneeled on patterned mats blanketing the ground in front of the cookfire. A few coals still burned, red and glaring against the shadows all around.

All around and above them, Marisians stepped out of the darkness. They were barefoot, their hair shorn close to the scalp so nothing could tangle in the water below. Their shoulders were broad, supporting impossibly barreled chests. Each one wore a necklace woven of clever knots and dangling shells. The weave tightened as it stretched over the torso and down to the tops of the knees.

Griffin tilted his head back to look into their faces. Though Somnites were pale, and Vineans had those bright green veins, the people from those worlds still looked human. Not the Marisians. They seemed ill at ease on their feet, like seals or penguins far more comfortable beneath the water. Their skin was a deep bronze, and it was tough, even the children's roughened by the sun and salt water.

The woman placed a hand over the shell-and-bone necklace that cut across her collarbone. "I am Seiche, and this is Guyot."

She placed five cups on the mat and dropped a pinch of green into each while Katherine introduced her husband and son. Guyot lifted a kettle off the coals and poured a stream of water over the herbs. Steam rose into the space between the people from Earth and those from Maris. Griffin shivered despite the warm night air.

A frown crossed Seiche's face. "It would be easier if we could see you."

Griffin glanced around him. "How about blankets?" All eyes dropped to him, or at least to the space around his head. "I mean, you've got blankets in your hammocks. If we pulled them over our shoulders, you'd see our outline at least."

Philip ruffled Griffin's hair. "Good thinking."

Seiche made a flicking motion with her hand, and someone in the crowd behind them dropped three blankets over the Fenns' shoulders.

"That's better." Guyot pressed his lips together. "You said you came to ask something of us."

Philip cleared his throat. "The song of the sea. On Caligo, we read that it protects you from the priests' magic. On other worlds, when a priest speaks, it takes hold of a person's mind, wipes it clean of any will but what that priest wishes. Our world, Earth, is in danger—we have no song, or anything like it. What we do have is highly trained soldiers, and they are being stolen by the priests and taken to other worlds to fight Somni's battles. We fear not only for our home, but for any world that might stand against the priests."

Seiche and Guyot exchanged a bewildered glance. "But the song is not ours to give."

Griffin's heart sank. Sweat broke out on his upper lip. Had they come all this way for nothing?

Guyot raised the steaming cup to his lips and the rest followed. Gasps and dark whispers filled the

air as the cups for the Fenn family rose into the air
without any visible hands to guide them, then tipped
back, the liquid disappearing into thin air.

Guyot frowned. "You would need to ask the
Guardian."

"And he is?"

"Not he. *It* lives far beneath the surface, where
the song is safe from invaders."

"What do you mean? The song is here, above the
water. I can hear it right now."

"Certainly. The song rises into the air just as it
flows beneath the surface. It lives all around us.
But all sound begins somewhere. Words start as
breath moving past vocal cords. Thunder travels
through the sky long before it ever reaches our ears.
A mother's call to her calf shifts and modulates as
it passes through the depths. The song is no different. Each phrase begins as a single note departing
the Guardian's chamber. As it journeys, it modulates,
picking up speed and resonance, building to its own
sentient self."

Sentient? The song was alive?

"Can you take us to this guardian?" Katherine
asked.

"Even if we agreed, it's impossible." Seiche
shrugged, the shells draped around her neck tinkling

as she moved. "You would not survive the journey."

"Impossible? Why?"

"The Guardian's chamber is far below the surface, much farther than people who are not of this world can dive." She cocked her head to the side. "Though the boy could do it, possibly."

"That's true." Guyot ran a hand along his jaw. "Until our young build up the necessary strength in their lungs, we secure air-filled bulbs over their heads when they dive. The bulbs aren't large enough for an adult head to fit inside. But the boy may be able to do it."

Beside him, Griffin could feel his mother begin to tremble. The air beneath the low roof shifted, her raw emotion speaking more profoundly than any of her words could. "No way is Griffin going down into some creature's lair without us."

Philip's voice sounded equally shaky. "Absolutely not. I'll go. Give me time—I can build up the stamina. I'll learn to hold my breath long enough."

"No." Guyot was firm. "Your being here endangers all of us. You cannot remain on Maris the months or years it would take you to learn our way of diving."

"We don't have months," Katherine murmured. She draped a protective arm over Griffin's shoulders. "But—you're sure there's no other way?"

Seiche and Guyot nodded in unison. "You'll need to hide during the day. We can't risk raising the soldiers' suspicions. After midnight tomorrow, either the boy travels below to the Guardian's chamber or the three of you leave this world. The decision is yours."

GRIFFIN

GRIFFIN WOKE WITH a start. He clawed at the netting over his face, straining for a full breath. His parents jerked awake and began pulling him free of the tangles. They'd slept for a few hours beneath the nets in case a patrol came along in the middle of the night. They didn't fully trust the crypsis juice to hide them—not while they were defenseless.

Griffin had thrashed all night, dreaming that he was drowning. He knew his parents would do everything they could so he didn't have to dive alone to get the song. But he also knew that if there wasn't another way, he'd have to do it, no matter how much the thought terrified him.

The air smelled like salt, and the song, cheerful as a morning greeting, rose above the waves slapping against the docks. Half the hammocks were empty, and a dozen Marisians crouched around the cookfire, gulping down a bright green porridge.

Griffin sat up. *"Pssttt!"*

A boy sitting with his back to them jumped, eyeing the lump of netting suspiciously.

"Is it safe to come out?"

The boy peered over his shoulder at the soldiers gathered around the launch, watching the boats ride the waves below. He beckoned, and the Fenns tiptoed after him. The Marisians around the cookfire watched the air where they passed with wary eyes. Griffin didn't blame them. He didn't think he'd ever get used to not being able to see his own arms and legs and everything else.

Seiche stood. "Follow me. Step *exactly* in my footsteps. And do not make a sound."

She strode out from under the cover of the broad roof and the Fenns hurried to follow. It was a shock, in the bright light of day, to turn in a full circle and see nothing but water. Shafts of sunlight pierced low-lying clouds. In the distance, a net of bubbles rose from the deep, the creature who'd set the trap snapping his massive jaws as he broke the surface.

The day had barely begun, but the docks already teemed with workers. They hefted thick ropes, hand over hand, lifting woven baskets out of the sea. Water spilled over the edges, sluicing off the glistening seaweed trapped within. The baskets were dumped into wide barrels where Marisian children stomped the seaweed into pulp like grapes in a vineyard. Green juice trickled out of a spout at the bottom. Griffin tiptoed past workers huddled over the drainpipes, siphoning the liquid into bladders, sealing them with a deft twist, and tossing them into a heap.

They passed a guard station, and Griffin held his breath the whole way, stepping as silently as he could. The soldiers glared as Seiche passed, but their eyes skimmed over the space behind her, where the three Fenns walked. Griffin risked a glance over his shoulder, ready to run if the soldiers had somehow seen them.

Maris was nothing like Somni. But the feeling of the place—the texture of fear that lay beneath everything, the hunched shoulders, the darting glances, the brooding reek of oppression—was exactly the same.

Seiche stepped to the edge of the docks and paused, waiting for them to catch up. Griffin peered over the side. The waves rolled by, the crests as little as five feet below, and the troughs as much as twenty. Without a word, Seiche rolled off the edge and out of sight. Griffin scrambled to see where she'd gone. A ladder clung to the pillar, descending into the water below. Seiche dropped, hand over hand, until first her feet, then her hips, then all of her was swallowed by the ocean.

Before he could chicken out, Griffin gripped the ladder and swung over the side. The waves rose to swat against his feet, and then they fell away, leaving a dizzying drop below. He hurried down before the thought of the next wave smashing against the ladder could stop him. Seiche had left the ladder for a horizontal rope and was quickly shimmying toward the aquaculture beds. The kelp stretched deep into the water, alternately floating weightless or hanging limp, dripping as the waves rolled by. The beaches back home were always littered with seaweed after a storm, feathery fronds and long whiplike ropes. But like everything on Maris, this kelp was so much bigger. The bulbs were lime green, and big as basketballs.

Griffin braced himself against the ladder as a wave crested, the water flooding up to his neck and the spray slapping his cheeks. Rather than giving in to the panic, he used it, launching off the ladder and, hand over hand, moving as fast as he could. Seiche watched the rope jangle as Griffin and his parents climbed across.

"It's safe to talk here," she said in a low voice. "The soldiers never get in the water. The few who have—well, let's just say it isn't only the human occupants of this world who want them gone."

"Mom? Dad?" Griffin said, breathless, as he wrapped his arms and legs around thick ropes of kelp.

"We're right behind you."

"Good," Seiche said. "Follow me."

She climbed up until she found a break in the kelp. She slid through, first one layer, then the next, and the one after that. When they passed through the last layer, they stepped into an open column leading down. The water below swished gently, the layers of kelp breaking the powerful waves. It would have been dark, except a second kind of seaweed grew between the thicker kelp, its delicate bulbs emitting a soft lavender light. The docks groaned above their heads, and here, so close to the water, the song softened, like a whisper from a friend.

Seiche dropped into the water, her arms and legs shifting into rhythmic swirls that kept her torso upright. Griffin took a breath and jumped, landing beside her. When his head broke the surface, he shook the water from his hair and blinked the salt from his eyes. His parents splashed down on either side of him. Seiche lifted down three bulbs tethered to the interior frame of the aquaculture beds and held them out so Griffin and his parents could each take one.

"These have been clipped from the ends of the kelp, then stretched and dried, just for this purpose." She inserted both her hands into the base and splayed her fingers wide. "Place it over your head and gently stretch. If you go slowly, it will seal around your neck. If you try to stretch it too far, it will rip."

She quirked an eyebrow as first Katherine, then Philip tried to stretch the bulbs over their foreheads. Katherine's split down the middle when she slid it past her nose. Philip couldn't even fit his over his forehead before it tore in several places.

Griffin's mouth went dry. Seiche was right—it really was up to him. He climbed up the frame just far enough that he could breathe without treading water. He lifted the bulb over his head and worked it down, first to his forehead, then below his nose, and finally past his chin. The lip settled over his neck. It was tight, and he fought against it, his breath coming fast and hard.

With the bulb over Griffin's head, for the first time Seiche was able to look directly at him while she spoke. "Breathe slowly, and calmly as you can. There's enough oxygen in there to get you to the

Guardian's chamber, where there is plenty of air. But if you panic, you'll use it up too quickly. It's a long dive down."

That only made it harder for Griffin to breathe. It took everything he had not to rip the thing off his head.

"The air inside the bulb will fight you as you descend, so take some time now to practice grabbing the rungs and pulling yourself down as quickly as you can."

Griffin slid back into the water until his eyes were level with the surface. Just as Seiche had instructed, he grabbed the frame and tugged downward. The light under the water was different, softer, and the song shifted too. Before he knew it, the fear was forgotten. It didn't feel dangerous underwater—it felt like sinking into a familiar dreamscape.

That is, until he felt his parents' hands grip him under the arms and drag him back up. When he broke the surface, the bulb was torn away from his face. But he wasn't gasping for air. He wasn't afraid anymore.

"Seiche?"

"Yes, Griffin?"

"Can I bring the song back in one of these bulbs? Would that even work?"

Seiche's face was impassive, her voice flat. "It is

highly unlikely that the Guardian will grant your request in the first place. *If* he does, you can be sure that he wouldn't release the song into anything but the most secure receptacle."

"Oh." Griffin's newfound confidence began to ebb.

"This is crazy," Philip said. "There has to be another way."

"It's okay, Dad. I'll be all right."

"No, Griffin," Katherine said. "It's too dangerous."

"Mom, come on. You know we don't have a choice."

There was no backup plan. All the worlds would fall under Somni control if someone didn't stop the priests. Apparently, that someone was him.

GRIFFIN

THE DAY PASSED while the Fenn family stayed hidden. As the sun set, sending ripples of pink and orange across the sky, Griffin's nerves began to get the best of him. He'd lived by the ocean his whole life, but he'd never done anything like an open water dive, much less in the dark. Seiche insisted that they wait until midnight, when the last patrols had bedded down for the night.

"I don't like it," Philip muttered. "Are you sure about this?"

"I'm sure." Griffin clenched his jaw so his teeth wouldn't rattle together. He wasn't sure, not at all, but it wouldn't help anything to let his parents know how scared he really was.

When the time came to go, Guyot stepped

forward, holding out a hand for Griffin. A half dozen Marisians peeled back the mats in front of the hearth and then lifted away a block of decking as big as a jeep. Below, the water sloshed, hemmed in on all sides by the rigid interior frame of the aquaculture beds. Guyot handed a bulb to Griffin, who stretched it down his face, stopping above his lips.

Seiche shepherded them to the edge. "There is a ladder leading down. If you stay at the center of the aquaculture beds, you'll be protected from the currents and any predators hunting tonight."

Griffin backed away from the edge, even his toes curling away from the water. He eyed the thrashing ocean below. He hadn't thought about predators. Guyot jumped through the hole in the decking, disappearing below the surface with a practiced kick. Griffin's parents fell to their knees and flung their arms around him. He hugged them back, as tight as he could.

"I love you guys." And because he was sure he'd lose his nerve if he waited another second, Griffin pulled away, sucked in one last deep breath, yanked the bulb below his chin, and dropped into the water.

He hit the surface with a splash and sank slowly down. It wasn't cold, but it was a shock all the same. The water closed over his head and the song changed.

The melody wasn't any different, but the texture was muted. It cradled him, coaxing away the fear that threatened to choke off his breath.

He wished his parents could be with him. He wished Fi were there. She would have adored the underwater plants. She would have loved the job only they could do. He wouldn't be scared at all if she were there.

Griffin kicked over to the wall of seaweed, pulling himself down the stiff frame, his ears popping as the pressure increased. He followed Guyot, trying to match the Marisian's confident strokes. By the time they were halfway down the structure, the bottom dropped out below, with nothing but the dark sea beneath them. Dread eclipsed everything else, and Griffin began to swim faster, flailing as panic seeped in.

But as they swam nearer the bottom, Griffin realized it wasn't just ocean down there. A murky *something* floated below the aquaculture beds. Spots wavered across his vision. Faster. He had to move faster. Guyot's fluttering kicks swept and swirled the water behind him and Griffin focused on that, drawing himself toward the shadow.

His lungs strained for air. The water seemed to grow thicker, fighting his every move. His fingers lost their grip. The edges of his vision blurred, shadows creeping in. But then Guyot was in front of him, shouting, pressing his face into the bulb over Griffin's head. Griffin tried to move his arms, to do whatever it was the Marisian wanted him to, but his limbs were stone. They were useless.

His eyes drifted closed. As water streamed past his fingers, a distant corner of Griffin's mind decided he must be drifting, let loose on the current below the farthest reach of the aquaculture beds. But then, he'd have to be moving against the current to feel the water rushing through his fingertips.

Guyot's grip bit into his skin as he dragged Griffin toward the shadow. And then, *pop*, he was falling. Not through the water, but into air. He landed on something squishy that gave and rebounded, spreading outward in a wet ripple. Guyot kneeled over him, a wicked-looking knife slicing at the bulb over Griffin's head. One minute Griffin was sure he was dying, and the next he was gulping in great lungfuls of air.

He rolled onto his back, panting for breath, his arms flung outward. His palms landed in something sticky. It seemed like all of him was draining—water seeping out of his clothes, out of his hair, out of his skin. Griffin's breath slowed. His pulse calmed its racing. The ceiling above shimmered a midnight blue, undulating with the waves that skimmed over it.

Oh. This chamber was the shadow. And he was *inside* that shadow.

The song had changed again—it was thinner, and more . . . *true* here. Like the difference between a sky so full of stars they all blur into a web of light, and when the first star of the night stands alone against a blanket of dark, bright and crisp and so very clear.

Guyot glanced up, then began backing away.

"Where are you going?"

"It is not . . . *comfortable* to be in the Guardian's presence."

"So you're leaving?"

"It's coming."

"It?"

Guyot didn't answer. He didn't look uncomfortable; he looked terrified.

Slowly, Griffin lumbered to his feet. The chamber was shallow but long. It was like standing on a jellyfish the size of a runway. The ground jiggled where his feet touched down, a dark iridescence mimicking the water below.

In the distance, so far away Griffin couldn't make out where the chamber ended and *it* began, something wiggled closer. It was as big as a bus and blurry at the bottom, as if a hundred wiggling legs moved it forward. Griffin froze. What *was* that? He'd only just gotten his breath back and already it felt like his heart was going to bang right out of his chest.

Guyot backed awkwardly toward the chamber wall, bending in half in a series of deep bows. He slid one hand between seams in the chamber wall, bracing his legs against the floor as first his arm, then his shoulder, then half of his torso sank into the wall. He gulped a breath, his ribs swelling like a balloon, then he thrust his face into the seam. With one last, powerful kick, Guyot's hips and legs slid through the seam and he was gone.

"Thanks," Griffin muttered. *I think.*

He turned to face whatever it was that shimmied closer, the slithering, creeping, far-too-big *something*. It had a bulbous head with wide, clicking eyes on either side and undulating tentacles that drew it along the ground like an enormous octopus. Griffin took a tentative step forward, the ground wobbling and jiggling beneath him like an anemone. He'd only gone a few steps when a deep voice rang out.

This is a first for both of us, Earth-child.

Griffin stopped midstride. He clamped his hands over his ears. That voice was in his head. Not like a memory, or a song you can't forget. It was inside his mind, poking around in there.

You were expecting a human like yourself to barter with. Don't be surprised—of course I know what it is you want. Tell me, would you trust something so sacred as the ocean's song to a human? The creature's thoughts probed Griffin's brain. Its tentacles swelled and slumped in what looked a lot like a shrug.

No, I thought not. Then why should I entrust you with the magic of this world?

Griffin opened his mouth, only to close it again. How could he put into words everything those priests had put his family through? And how close they were to losing each other again? Griffin winced. "Go ahead, look for yourself."

There was a long pause while the creature filtered through his memories: his thoughts and his secrets, the loneliness and the grief. His mom and dad, missing, then found. And Fi. On a different world, in a danger he couldn't help her face. The chamber was silent except for the swishing of the water above and the water below, and the song that permeated everything on this world.

I see. The voice was strained. *Still, I cannot give you what you ask.*

Griffin blanched. "But—after everything—you're just going to let them win?"

You believe that our song will free all the worlds, yet Maris only wishes to be left alone. We want nothing to do with your wars. We have suffered enough.

"None of us want this!" Griffin sputtered. "You can't be impartial, not now. None of us can. War is coming for all of the worlds, whether we want it or not." He braced himself for the intrusion, for the tendrils wiggling through his mind like the tentacles that coiled out from the creature's bulbous body. "Look again."

Griffin scrunched his eyes shut. He called up memory after memory, of the fight to rescue his dad, of his mom in chains deep in the bowels of the rectory, of the people stolen from each world, suspended in the priest's temple, tubes siphoning off their dreams and draining the life from their bodies.

Griffin felt the creature latch on to that memory, reel it back and play it again—the moment when Griffin had risked everything to try unhooking the elderly, feeble Marisian man so he could find his way home again.

The creature snapped each of its tentacles tight to its body like so many snakes recoiling. Colors rippled over its skin, furious reds and bruising purples.

You tried to free him.

"Yes."

A Way between Worlds

You might have been caught. Your pursuers were close behind, and soldiers before.

"I'd do it again. It doesn't matter what world we're from. If we don't stand together, sooner or later they'll come for us all."

The Guardian watched Griffin, the reds and purples rolling down its arms beginning to pale and slow to a crawl. At length, it stretched one tentacled arm along the chamber wall. Its suction cup pulsed as it drew an iridescent orb from the membrane. The ocean's song swelled, gathering in strength until it simmered at the edges of Griffin's every sensation. The creature released the orb, sending it toward Griffin in a boneless ripple. He opened his hands and the orb touched down on the pads of his fingers, trembling as it settled there.

The orb shrank in his hands, tightening in on itself until it was no bigger than a ball, then a peach, then a pearl, the song shrinking with it as it hardened, holding its new shape. The pearl hummed, the song trapped inside vibrating through his palm and down the length of his arm.

Griffin stared at the shimmering thing in wonder. "Thank you," he breathed.

But he didn't have a pouch to tuck it into. Or a sock. Or anything, for that matter. He didn't trust the spider silk clothing not to lose it. Reluctantly, he opened his mouth, tucking the pearl beneath his tongue. It tasted like salt, and it softened again as it settled in, latching there like a living thing. Griffin swallowed gingerly, but the pearl didn't move.

The creature extended a tentacled arm again, this time pushing a much larger bubble out of the chamber wall. It bobbed, wobbling with the current, ready to tug free at any moment.

Hurry, now. Step inside, and this vessel will carry you to the surface again.

Griffin lumbered forward, his steps awkward on the wriggling, rippling chamber floor. "Thank you—I can't tell you how much—"

Don't thank me. Only guard the song well. The wicked ones must not capture even one note.

Griffin clambered inside the bubble. "I'll keep it safe. I promise."

The seam closed in front of his eyes and the bubble separated from the chamber wall. Griffin pressed himself against the edge, watching the creature grow smaller and smaller. As it was tugged into the current, the bubble rose slowly toward the surface and away from the aquaculture beds, until the creature was nothing more than a smudge on the larger shadow of the chamber.

A school of fish with teeth like hedge trimmers swam straight toward him, fighting the current, their tails swishing side to side, bumping into the bubble and sending it spinning. Griffin braced his palms against the sides. When the last fish passed, it swatted the bubble away like an inner tube in a waterpark. Griffin spun, screaming like he was on a roller coaster ride that just went from fun-scary to flat-out terrifying. When the bubble finally slowed, bobbing upright, Griffin strained for a glimpse of the glowing aquaculture beds.

He couldn't see them anywhere. He was lost. Griffin's fingertips began to prickle, his hair standing up on end. How long would he be floating before someone found him? It wouldn't matter that he'd gotten the song if he couldn't find his way home again.

A second school of curious fish swam past Griffin, ghostly white, their glossy eyeballs the most substantial thing about them. They wound around the bubble in acrobatic figure eights and darted away as quickly as they had appeared.

Eventually, the ocean around him paled as the surface beckoned. A boat sliced through the water above. It was moving fast, propelled by a stiff wind. In its wake, a host of floating creatures like jellyfish bobbed, their colorful ribbons trailing deep into the water below.

Griffin flinched away from the ribbons that slid over the bubble like the tails of a thousand kites, tugging at its edges. As the bubble wobbled higher, the ribbons became thicker and tacky, the jellies clutching their catch as the current rushed past.

Griffin swallowed his panic. Should he cut through the bubble and try to escape? But what if the jellyfish were poisonous? Griffin peered overhead—the surface seemed so close, as if he could stretch out his hand and touch it. And then, suddenly, his ears popped. Water flowed under and beside the bubble, and above, there was nothing but sky. Griffin reached up, peeling at the membrane until he broke through, thrusting his head and shoulders out the top, and drinking in glorious gulps of fresh air.

Dawn broke, the first rays of morning light streaming over the waves. The water was warm, but the air was crisp. Griffin turned to face the wind rushing past him, carrying the storm clouds on the horizon closer. The jellies beneath him were like a living raft, the ribbons in the water tethering their insubstantial bodies to the surface, the smaller ones rippling steadily, front to back, propelling the raft forward, toward a familiar shadow in the distance, toward the aquaculture beds.

GRIFFIN

GRIFFIN CLIMBED ONTO the docks, swaying a little as he found his footing on the wet planks. Though it was barely morning, the docks were already a flurry of activity. Marisians stoked the cookfire beneath the thatched roof, dove below to inspect the aquaculture beds, and tossed nets into the water from the docks above, the patrolling Somni soldiers watching their every move.

"Hey!"

Griffin froze.

"You, there!"

Griffin didn't turn around. The Marisian mending nets down the dock from him had gone stiff, her eyes wide. She looked over Griffin's shoulder at the soldier he'd just passed. Was water dripping off him and leaving marks on the docks? Were his footsteps making too much noise?

Griffin looked down. His arms and legs were flickering into view—splotches of his skin mirrored the sea behind him, but other sections were back to his own pale coloring. Was the crypsis juice wearing off already?

The Marisian dropped the nets in her hands and lifted the bone strung around her neck up to her lips. Her cheeks puffed and released their breath forcefully, but the whistle made no sound that Griffin could hear.

"Get back in the water," she whispered.

"But my parents—" Behind Griffin, footsteps pounded against the docks.

The Marisian shook her head in a tight jerking motion. "Go!" She darted forward and shoved Griffin off the dock. He fell backward, his arms and legs flailing through the long drop down to the waves below. It was all he could do to keep from screaming before he hit the water.

Panic stole his breath and the waves swallowed him. Bubbles of air spilled off his skin, making a break for the surface. Griffin thrashed, straining to find the way up, but everything was churning, swirling around him. Prisms of sunlight reached for him and Griffin swam toward the sky. The last bits of air trickled out of his nostrils as he broke the surface. He treaded water, gasping and casting around to get his bearings.

Where were his mom and dad? Had the soldiers found them? Were they adrift on the waves just like him? Much as he wanted to kick up out of the water and scale the pillar to the elevated docks to search for them, Griffin kept his head low, hoping the last of the crypsis juice would hide him from the soldiers.

Three boats dropped into the water, paddles spinning, spitting water as they cut through the waves, straight toward him. Griffin sucked in a breath and dipped his head under, darting to the side as if he were fighting against a rip current. He kicked like a frog, pumping his arms as fast as he could, cursing the woman on the docks for dumping him in the water like that. He might have stood a chance on solid ground. He didn't have lungs like a Marisian, or layers of blubber.

Griffin glanced behind him. Three narrow hulls sliced through the water, way too close. He had to get another breath without the soldiers spotting him. Griffin flipped onto his back, letting his head float upward until his face broke through the water. He gulped a breath and then wriggled back down, wasting precious energy trying to hide and swim at the same time.

Again, he dove away from the oncoming boats, but he only got a few kicks in before he needed to breathe again. This time, they were so close that even if the crypsis juice was still working, they'd see the water parting, and hear him gasping for air.

"There!" one of the soldiers shouted, pointing as Griffin's lips broke the surface. The boats turned as smoothly as jet skis and bore down on him.

Griffin's heart sank. His best chance—his only chance—was to let the boats get close, then dive once they were almost on top of him. Even that would only hold them off for a moment. He couldn't keep it up forever.

They had him. It was over.

Fi would never let the priests and their soldiers catch her, not without a fight. If she was going down, she'd take them all with her. Griffin drew in a deep breath and sank. Maybe his parents had gotten away. He could give them one more minute, at least. He beat his arms and, once he was far enough down to flip over, flutter-kicked his legs, driving himself as deep as he could go.

The boats screamed by overhead before spinning around and circling above the spot where he'd disappeared. Griffin let out one more burst of kicks before he leveled out, his lungs begging for air. He squinted up through the layers of dark, the bubbles streaming out of his nose wobbling steadily upward. His fingers flicked as the currents teased past them. This was it. Griffin fluttered his eyelashes, the salt water stinging his eyes. Now that he'd stopped fighting it, his body rose slowly to the surface.

Softly at first, then more insistently, a familiar clicking tapped against his eardrums, sounding along the length of his body. Griffin closed his eyes. It was probably only his oxygen-deprived mind, desperate for something to cling to. With a last gust of effort, Griffin beat at the water until he was stretched flat, his arms held wide, hands cupped, waiting. A soft shadow swam beneath him, brushing against his belly and lifting his weightless body onto its back.

With a questioning chirrup, the ray slotted Griffin's hands onto the base of its wings. The boats churned above, Griffin's lungs screamed for air, and the giant ray shot forward, launching out of the water, carrying Griffin safely on its back.

He gasped for breath, shaking wet clumps of hair out of his eyes. On the horizon, another giant ray leaped out of the water, Katherine clinging to its back. Griffin cried out in relief. He glanced behind him. *Dad?* But all he saw were the boats spinning around to begin their chase, a steady line closing in on the rays, their numbers swelling until it seemed as if the whole Somnite army was after him.

With a chirrup of glee, a third ray broke the surface. Philip gripped the ray's fins, struggling to hold on as the boats closed in, their bows nipping at the ray's kitelike tail. Griffin jerked his head back around just as his ray dipped below the water again. Griffin squeezed his eyes shut against the water rushing over his face and down the length of his body, leaving his feet fluttering behind.

Griffin hung on, struggling to breathe when they broke the water, and then to fight the urge to black out when they plunged under again. The soldiers were so close, if he lost his grip now, he'd tumble straight into the oncoming boats. The rays swam toward the lighthouse buoy where it rocked in the waves, the red roof swinging side to side.

The spray from the waves crashing against the base of the buoy slapped against the gallery window high above. The first ray carrying Katherine leaped out of the water directly in front of the tower, swiveling in the air just as it had when the Fenns first arrived on Maris. Katherine let go as the ray soared overhead, dropping onto the buoy at the base of the tower and rolling until she came to a stop inches from the edge.

"Mom!" Griffin screamed.

She stumbled to her feet, beckoning and shouting, holding one arm close against her body and limping a little. Griffin gulped a breath as the ray dipped under, diving deep this time, pumping its wings furiously to build speed. They tore out of the water, the ray chirruping as it began to twist in the air.

The tower loomed, teetering in the waves. Griffin cringed even as he got his feet under him to spring away from the ray's back. Panic closed off his throat. His heart pounded in his chest. He couldn't do this. He was going to smack against that wall and then it wouldn't matter how close behind the soldiers were. He couldn't make it. He couldn't.

The ray was nearly sideways, its wings fluttering in the breeze that sheered off the tips of the waves. And there, standing at the edge of the buoy, was Griffin's mom: arms outstretched, eyes locked on her son, determined to keep him from falling.

Griffin let go. The ray spun away from him, careening toward the welcoming water. Griffin kicked, flailing to keep himself upright, bracing for the *thud*. But somehow, he landed on his feet, running, his hands flying up to shield his face. Just as he was about to smash into the bricks, wiry arms broke his fall, holding tight as he crashed toward the ground.

Griffin rolled, and his mom rolled with him. When they came to a stop, she only gripped him tighter. "You're okay," she yelled above the roar of the waves and the song of the sea. "I've got you."

Katherine's cheek streamed with blood. Griffin's right leg and arm were on fire, the skin scraped and raw. But they were alive. Katherine helped Griffin to his feet.

"You got the song?"

Griffin nodded. The pearl was still there, lodged in the soft folds between his tongue and jaw.

"Then go!" She nudged him toward the door. "I'll wait for your father."

"But what if opening the portal works differently here?"

Katherine wicked a trail of water out of her eyes. "It may. But the Levitator will pull us through."

"You don't know that, Mom."

"Griffin, please go. I might be wrong, but if they catch us, at least we tried everything we could."

"I'm staying with you."

"No." Katherine gripped the sides of Griffin's face, pressing her forehead against his. "This is bigger than your father and me. We *have* to get that song to Earth. Everything depends on this."

The boats circled the base of the tower, fighting against the waves. One of the soldiers tossed a line over the railing to anchor the boat to the buoy. Katherine yanked herself away from her son and darted forward, throwing the grappling hook back at the soldiers who ducked out of the way, cursing.

"Look," Katherine shouted, pointing. "He's almost here. Now go!"

The ray carrying his dad broke the water, twisting as it hurtled toward them. She was right. They just might make it. Griffin flung open the door and tore up the stairs, fighting against the violent swaying of the tower as the waves rolled past. He made it to the first floor landing and hung on while the ground beneath him lurched.

As the buoy rocked back toward its center, Griffin raced up in a flurry of steps, then held on, bracing as the tower leaned out over the water again. When the ground leveled out, he burst upward in another sprint. When he reached the watch room, he hollered, "Hey! Hey Levitator—you'd better be listening. You promised!"

Nothing happened. He lay flat on the ground, wrapping his arms and legs around the railing. "You get my family out of this, or I swear I am coming through that portal and I am going to—"

"Griffin!"

He crawled across the floor and peered over the edge. His mom and dad sprinted up the spiral stairs. They didn't have time to wait out the worst of the rocking like Griffin had—they were thrown all over the staircase as they climbed, knocked into the brick wall and then the wrought iron railing as the lighthouse swung back and forth.

"Hurry!" he yelled.

Not ten steps behind them, the soldiers pounded up the stairs. Griffin faced the bull's-eye, ready to scream again for the Levitator. But he didn't need to. The lens had stopped swiveling—which it never did, day or night, unless someone was opening the portal. The brick walls began to hum, then rattle, and finally the bull's-eye began to spin in a viscous swirl.

The Levitator had heard them.

Katherine made it to the lantern room and lunged for Griffin's hand. She reached the other down toward Philip. "Now!" she yelled.

Philip strained, wincing in pain as he leaped up the last few steps. He clasped Katherine's hand and together the three of them dove straight toward the open portal even as it reached out to draw them in. Philip's skin fizzled translucent, and then Katherine's, but before the portal grabbed Griffin, he was tackled in midair, his hand wrenched out of his mom's grip. He smacked against the floor. The soldier who'd brought him down shoved Griffin's face into the cold, hard steel.

26

FI

IT WAS ALWAYS dizzying, every single time Fi shot through the portal. When she found her feet, she knew without opening her eyes that she'd landed on Somni. She could smell it—the dry air catching in her mouth and sucking away all the moisture. But more than that, she could feel the absence of the green like a hitch in her breath, a hole in her chest. A moan slipped through her lips as the ache of being without it settled into its familiar place.

When her eyes fluttered open, she darted back, her hands braced against the gallery windows. Guards filled the watch room below, lining the stairs leading up to where she stood, weapons trained on her. But those weren't soldiers' stolas they wore.

And something else was different, though it took her a moment to place what, exactly, had changed. The peppery remnant of the priests' magic that had always clung to the air was gone, and in its place wafted the heady scent of sap.

The guard directly in front of Fi propped his staff against the railing and raised his arms in a gesture of goodwill. "We have no fight with Vinea. We're not going to hurt you."

Fi wasn't often shocked into silence—but after years spent alternately loathing and fearing the Somnite guards, welcome was the last thing she'd expected. Her eyes dropped to his chest. *Oh.* Glass pendants hung around each of the guards' necks. They weren't soldiers at all.

The guards were ordinary citizens of Somni, the sjel tree essence inside the glass shielding them from the priests' control. Either Griffin or his dad had made those pendants. A wave of gratitude washed over Fi. Even though he was worlds away, Griffin was still here with her, in a way.

She straightened out of her defensive crouch. "I've come back for the raze crews."

The guards exchanged a look, and finally the one who'd spoken before crossed to the gallery door and opened it, motioning for Fi to step through. "See for yourself. After the priests left, the raze crews made their way to the temple."

Fi stepped onto the gallery, and out into the sharp yellow air. She leaned against the railing and peered down into the amphitheater below. Hundreds of Vineans huddled together. Fi's heart caught in her throat. *Hundreds.* "What are they waiting for? Why didn't they go home as soon as they were free?"

The guard shrugged. "I guess they're waiting for someone to come get them. So many are elderly, and all of them are weak. The priests worked those raze crews near to death. We didn't want to send them through the portal into the thick of the fighting."

The guard fidgeted, his eyes finding anything but her own.

"What is it?"

"Somni is running out of food. The priests cut off shipments from the aquaculture beds on Maris, and our gardens can only produce so much. They're trying to starve us out." The guard's face went tight. "The raze crews have suffered terribly at Somnite hands. It doesn't feel right, wishing for them to go. But if we had hundreds fewer mouths to feed, we might be able to hang on."

Fi turned back to the lantern room. Even if her

family was among the prisoners below—even if she'd finally found them—was she too late? "Then let me down there. I've come to take them home."

Again, the soldier raised his arms, almost pleading this time. "We have no fight with you, but we can't let you pass either."

"And why is that?"

"You understand—we must take precautions. We *just* got our world back, and we're barely hanging on to it. We can't let you pass."

Fi fumed. She'd come too far to let this be the end. It must have felt like this for Griffin, when all he'd wanted was to save his dad but he kept slamming up against one "no" after another. But he'd shown them, in the end. He'd forced Arvid to—

Wait.

"Send someone for Arvid. He'll vouch for me."

The Somnite guards exchanged a puzzled look, but they didn't move.

"What are you waiting for? Go!"

Fi whirled around. She darted back inside and hurried in the opposite direction of the lens's slow spin, searching for the bull's-eye to Caligo. When she found it, she slapped her hands against the greenish glass and shouted, "Hey! Are you listening to this?"

She pressed her face close to the glass, keeping

pace with the swiveling lens. "We're coming, hundreds of us. And you'd better be ready."

When she stepped away, the guards were all staring.

"The mists on Caligo are healing. And I'm not saying that eggy stuff they eat is any good, but they've got lots of it."

Arvid didn't look pleased to be hauled out of the dream caves below the city. When he was hustled to the top of the stairs, he sagged back against the railing. "I should have known," he said between breaths. He clapped the shoulder of the nearest guard. "She's a troublemaker all right, but it's the good kind of trouble, I suppose."

The guard backed out of Fi's way, extending an arm toward the stairs. "My apologies for the delay."

"Come on," Arvid called over his shoulder as he started back down the spiral stairs.

Fi shook her head as she followed close behind him, the guards stepping aside to let her pass. It was *too* strange—those faces had been her enemies for so long. And now they were helping her?

The temple looked nothing like the last time Fi had been there. The nave was silent except for the shushing of sandaled feet on worn brick. Half of the stone pews were overturned, some split down the middle. The alcoves that used to hold the stolen dreamers were empty, the tubes shredded so they could never be used again. Fi's breath caught in her throat and she looked away from the deep red stains in the brick.

Eb.

What had they done with all the dead?

Before she had the chance to ask, the temple doors were thrown wide. Yellow light streamed into the nave and Fi dashed toward it, the guards falling back as she broke into the open air and hurried down the temple steps.

Vineans filled the amphitheater. They looked lost, like refugees, unsure if they'd ever see home again. Together they swiveled to face her in an eerie echo of the priests' ceremony. Their stolas were filthy, the skin around their ankles scarred and angry. They had suffered so much for so long. Tears pricked Fi's eyes and anger boiled her insides, white-hot steam filling her lungs until she thought she would scream.

Whispers scattered across the crowd. "*Look.* Look at her veins."

"A greenwitch! A young greenwitch has come for us!"

And, then, from far away, "Fi?"

The whispers stopped.

"Fionna, is that you?"

The crowd parted and a small cluster of people approached. They moved slowly, holding one another up as they stumbled forward. Fi shielded her eyes as hope tamped down her anger, like a tight-fitting lid over a pot of simmering water. Their faces were drawn, their proud backs hunched. But it was them—her great-uncles Fin and Ira, her great-aunt Ela, and her aunts Gee and Nan.

The tears that had been jabbing at her eyelids burst out. Fi dropped her face into her hands and sobbed. *Five.* Before the soldiers tore her family apart, twelve of them had lived in the cave back on Somni. But somehow, impossibly, five of them were standing right in front of her.

They were alive.

Fi lurched forward, into their arms. They held her to them, one after another, and Fi felt with each embrace that she was holding them upright as much as they were holding her tight. When she pulled herself back at last, each one of her aunts and uncles wiped away tears.

"You're all right?" One by one she laid her palms against their weathered cheeks, peering into their eyes.

"We are now, child," Great-Aunt Ela's voice trembled.

"Come with me. Please? I'll take you somewhere you can rest."

Great-Uncle Fin's eyes hardened. "We can't rest, not yet—not until Vinea is free."

"Shouldn't we go straight there?" Aunt Gee asked.

Fi swallowed. "Yes, they need you on Vinea. But you can't help if you're this weak. We have to take care of you first."

Aunt Nan cupped a hand over Fi's cheek. "We trust you, Fionna dear."

Fi wrested herself away. She looked over her shoulder to the tower high above. There was no way they'd make it up the spiral stairs leading all the way to the lantern room. Fi called over to where the Somnite guards watched. "Can you carry them? We've got to get them to the portal."

Arvid shouted instructions and the guards hefted the frail raze crews onto their backs, then disappeared inside the temple. Fi darted ahead, sprinting up the tower stairs. Already, the bricks hummed with the opening of the portal. Fi leaped up the last flight, two at a time. When she reached the lantern room, the lens had stopped turning on its pedestal. The glass in the middle of the panel leading to Caligo stretched and began to twist.

Fi leaned over the railing. The spiral stairs were filled with people streaming steadily upward. "The portal's open!" she shouted. "Hurry!"

The next thing she knew, the spiral of liquid glass reached out toward her, thinning the edges of her skin until it glowed, translucent. With a tug at her insides and a roar of light, she left Somni behind.

27

FI

FI LANDED ON Caligo, the mists nipping at her arms like an old friend scolding her for falling out of touch. She shooed them away, but only enough so she had a good view of the portal. She stepped back, making room for the others who should be following her through at any moment.

"*Come on,*" she breathed. Or rather, she didn't breathe, not for the long, anxious seconds while she waited for something to happen. And then, suddenly, she wasn't alone in the lantern room anymore.

The Vineans landed on Caligo one by one. They stared in astonishment at the city in the sky. In turn, the mists welcomed them, spilling through cracks in the brick and seams in the window glazing to swirl around their broken bodies. Those with enough energy to descend the stairs followed Fi down and outside to the platform, where a steady stream of boats approached through the mists. Fi settled her family in the first two boats and hopped in after. The moment she was seated, the boat skipped gently forward, careful not to jostle its passengers.

Fi watched as her family took in the strange beauty of Caligo. Great-Uncle Fin leaned over the boat's edge, crying out in astonishment as a flying lizard, its scales shimmering green to gold, dove straight down, disappearing behind a layer of mist. Great-Aunt Ela peered around her, gripping the edges of the boat as if it might flip upside down at any moment.

Fi leaned forward, placing a gentle hand between her shoulder blades. "You're safe. Nothing can hurt you here."

Ela reached back and clasped Fi's hand in both of her own. "Bless you, child."

The people of Caligo had always seemed aloof to Fi, too accustomed to their thin air to care what happened on less fortunate worlds. But as the boats carrying the raze crews neared the aerie's broad platform, the entire fleet awaited them, ready to welcome the refugees. Maybe Fi had been too quick to judge them after all.

When the boats sidled up beside the platform,

she hopped out, helping her aunts and uncles to find their footing, and over to a table weighed down by food. The Levitator and his fleet scurried around, until every last Vinean had been seen to.

She kneeled at their feet, happy to watch their faces alight in wonder, to see them eat and drink, to know the mists were healing them with every passing second.

Aunt Gee fixed Fi with a knowing look. "Go on. Ask."

"How did you survive all those years? How can you smile, even now?" She shook her head. "It must have been terrible."

There was a long pause when no one answered. And then, softly, "It was."

Fi sat up straight. "Tell me."

Aunt Gee sighed. "We were captured, and then separated. That was the first horrible part. We didn't know what had happened to any of the others. We were each alone, wrecked by grief. When they first sent me to Somni, it felt like someone had sucked the marrow from my bones. I was broken, and not just my heart. All of me.

"But if you endure it long enough, even the worst place on all the worlds can seem normal. We got used to the soldiers. We adjusted to the chains around our ankles. We came to understand the barren ground."

"You weren't a servant, not even in the beginning?"

"No—those of us who fought capture were sent straight to the raze crews. They didn't trust us near their priests."

Fi twisted her hands in her lap. "But how did you bear it?"

The older woman looked down at her hands, scarred from years spent digging in unforgiving soil. "Sometimes things happen to a person—terrible, soul-crushing things. You'd never wish it on anyone, not even your enemies. But the upside to all that pain? You find a strength you never knew was possible. You learn things about yourself you'll only discover on the other side of suffering."

"Aunt Gee?"

"Yes, love?"

Fi bit her lip. It suddenly seemed foolish, how much hope she'd hung on a single recollection. "I have this memory. About you—about the raze crews. I think . . . Aunt Gee, is it possible that the raze crews know something the greenwitches don't?"

Aunt Gee raised an eyebrow, and she tilted her head to the side. She paused a long moment before she spoke. "It is."

A breath Fi hadn't realized she'd been holding

rushed out of her. "But—how? How is that possible?"

Aunt Gee leaned forward, brushing empty egg-shells out of the way and planting her elbows on the low table. She turned Fi's palm up, drawing a finger along the faintly glowing veins cutting across her wrist. "It isn't only you greenwitches who wield power. Every Vinean has a little green in their veins, do they not?"

Fi nodded, barely breathing.

"Because there was next to no green around us, we became more attuned to the little we held within us. After a time we discovered that we could use that tiny bit of green. On Somni, we were like seeds, gone dormant to protect ourselves. We found that we could ask small things of the seeds we encountered."

"But—not even greenwitches can do that. Not with seeds."

Aunt Gee nodded. "Those years on Somni changed us. They ground us down. We became feeble. But even so, we fought back, in our own way; in the only way we could. Do you know how many seeds we planted?"

Fi shook her head.

"Millions. Yes, we ripped up the plants like they told us to. But we also snipped off seed pods, stored them in our sashes, and breathed our wishes over them each night. The following day, when we dug our spades into the soil to rip a plant from the ground, we spilled a dozen seeds in its place."

"And?"

"We waited. Then, one day, we saw a signal flashing out of the tower—"

Fi smirked.

"That was you, wasn't it?" Aunt Gee chuckled. "We saw the signal, though we didn't know who had sent it, or why, and we called in our favor. As one, all those seeds burst through their hulls, sprouts climbing out of the ground, reaching for the air, searching out those who held us captive. Vines grew out of cracked soil, swallowing the soldiers and entombing them where they stood. We unlocked the horrid shackles around our ankles and simply walked free."

Fi breathed as hard as if she'd just finished sprinting up the tower steps. "Do you think—is it possible—if you come back to Vinea with me, could you do the same thing?"

A wry smile curved across Aunt Gee's lips. "I don't see why not."

28

FI

THE LEVITATOR INSISTED the weakest of the raze crews remain on Caligo to allow the mists to do their healing work. It was the right decision, of course, but when it came time to leave her family behind, Fi wept, her tears half joy and half sorrow. Their suffering was behind them, but she didn't know how she'd bear leaving them again so soon.

Aunt Gee and Aunt Nan, along with twenty others, traveled with her through the portal to Vinea. When they arrived on their home world, Fi's half-and-half tears were nothing compared to theirs. The Vinea they'd left had been under occupation by Somnite soldiers, but beyond the fort, the green had stubbornly held its own.

Not anymore. The line between what was left of

the wildlands and the burned ground stretched out before them, clear to the horizon. Fi gulped back the taste of bile on the back of her tongue and gritted her teeth against the headache that pounded between her temples.

"Fast as you can," she whispered, prodding them forward. "We have to get to the green so it can protect us."

Their first steps faltered, but they made their way down the spiraling stairs and halfway out of the fort before the soldiers on patrol spotted them. This time, Fi didn't even need to ask—the trees dropped their leaves, swirling around the soldiers, blinding them.

"Run!" Fi shouted.

They couldn't actually move at anything close to a run, but the green covered their passage until they reached the shoulder-high ferns beneath a stand of ash trees. The wildlands swallowed them, hiding their passage until they'd left the soldiers far behind. When Fi was certain the soldiers had lost their trail, she closed her eyes and let the green lead them to the outpost. It sheltered the travelers, easing their path forward, leaving pools of water and clusters of berries and root vegetables along the way.

Fi put her shoulders back, trying to silence the doubts that hounded her with every step. The umpteenth time she peered over her shoulder to check on Aunt Gee and Aunt Nan, the women shooed her away. "We're *fine*. We survived the raze crews. We're strong enough for this."

They pressed on, all of them, showing no sign of stopping, though their progress was painfully slow. After two days of travel overland, they arrived at the battle site. The outpost was abandoned, the resistance gone deep into hiding.

Fi cast around her, at a loss for how to begin. Twenty-three people, counting her. That was all they had against Somni's army. Had she only brought them here to die? Was she only prolonging the end of Vinea? Was it all for nothing?

No.

If Aunt Ada were here, she'd say that *she* believed in Fi. If Liv were here, she'd clap Fi on the back and tell her to do what needed doing, and well. If Griffin were here, he'd take her hand and walk with her, even if he didn't have the first clue what to do. Suddenly Fi didn't feel so alone, so much like she was setting out on a fool's errand.

She led the raze crews up the low rise to the copse of trees where they could see the soldiers guarding the camp in the distance. "The priests are there," she explained, "and the kidnapped Vinean children too."

"We're ready," Aunt Nan said.

Fi cleared her throat. "I can cover you—but you'll have to trust me. Stay close together. And keep walking forward, no matter what."

She didn't have to say it—she didn't need to ask for their trust. She already had it. The people who followed her had resigned themselves to never being freed, never coming home, never being able to fight against those who imprisoned them. She'd already done so much for them. They trusted her because she'd earned it.

Fi gathered the folds of her tunic into her fists and closed her eyes. The green leaped into her vision, stronger than it ever had—the lifeblood of the trees above, the ferns blanketing the ground, and the dense thicket like a rear guard at their flank. The green was so vivid she staggered back, and a dozen hands were there to catch her. With her eyes closed, she could see the soldiers, and the priests, and their prisoners within the walls of the camp.

When she was a little girl in hiding, Aunt Ada had told Fi about the marvel of living architecture—how the greenwitches had called up chapels and schools and bridges to span untouched swaths of the wildlands, and how the green had collapsed those bridges the moment the invaders had stepped onto them. All through her exile, Fi had lain in bed at night, trying to imagine wonders she thought she'd never witness.

Fi never dreamed she'd be the one to call something like that into being.

Shield us?

She stumbled, bracing herself against Aunt Nan as the green thundered into her, through her. The wildlands responded with an audible *whoosh*. She could feel the will of the green life all around her, and of the Vineans who came with her, lending her what strength they had. Sticks flew through the air, and logs thicker than her wingspan. Vines lashed it all together until a floating wall preceded the raze crews as they marched down the hill, toward those who had chained them for decades, who stood between them and freedom.

The soldiers' attack was ruthless. They gave no thought for their own safety, or for the violence in their hands—the priests had taken all their own thoughts from them. Against a human defense, the soldiers would have been unstoppable. But the green wall shifted and swelled to meet everything they threw at Fi and her companions. Fi had called the shield into being, but it had taken on a life of its own. Having finally been given a shape to fight Vinea's invaders, the green seized its chance to attack. The raze crews didn't need weapons, they didn't need a war cry; they simply walked with Fi up to the camp gates.

Fi didn't ask the gates to open. She didn't need to. Her will and the will of the green were the same. The wooden pikes surrounding the camp called on a trace of green at their cores and splintered until sawdust was all that remained of the priests' barricade. They had built their fortress from the very thing that would destroy them.

The raze crews swarmed the fort, their whispers filling Fi's mind. The seeds beneath the soil became their weapons, and they called up life from the ground beneath their feet. Tendrils snaked out of the ground, hunting down the priests in their red robes. They screamed, shouting commands, but their brainwashed soldiers could not protect them from this. The green poured out of the ground seed by seed until it covered the priests' mouths, closing off their throats and wringing the life from their bodies.

As the priests were snuffed out one by one, their hold on the soldiers snapped. The soldiers dropped their weapons, stumbling away and falling to the ground in horror at what they had been made to do. The green drained out of Fi, leaving her mind empty and every inch of her throbbing with spent power.

• • •

Days later, Fi was still too tired even to raise her head to look around the chapel where the resistance had gathered to see to their wounded and to care for the frightened children. Her aunts Ada, Gee, and Nan surrounded her. They swept the hair from her brow, lifted water to her lips to drink, and held her hand while she fell again into a deep sleep, not because of what she was or what she could do, but because she was their Fionna, and they loved her no matter what.

Melanie Crowder

GRIFFIN

THE GROUND BENEATH Griffin rocked gently. The ocean's song rolled past with the waves, keening softly in time with his throbbing heart. Griffin opened his eyes in a squint. The sun was high overhead. He could feel the pale skin of his face burning. His right cheek was swollen and aching, his lips cracked, the metallic tang of blood seeping into his mouth. Griffin swallowed. There, under his tongue, was something hard. A round, smooth *something* sticking stubbornly to his gums. The song.

Griffin's arms were strung up over his head, lashed to one of the pillars lifting the docks high above the water. His feet were bound too, his ankle-bones mashed painfully together. Griffin's chin dropped to his chest. He'd never felt so alone.

He'd been so close—seconds from escaping through the portal. At least his parents were together—and safe—for now. His eyes burned, and every inch of him ached. Footsteps pounded along the dock and Griffin bit down on his tongue, blinking back tears. He wouldn't cry in front of them. He would not.

The swaying red robes of a Somni priest wavered into view. Griffin turned his face away. A soldier grabbed his chin, forcing him to look up, but Griffin stared stubbornly at the button on the priest's collar, refusing to meet his eyes.

"You," the priest snarled. "We heard all about what you did on Somni."

Griffin sucked at his cheeks. He wouldn't say a word. He wouldn't help them, no matter what.

"Oh yes," the priest continued. "And I know all about your parents. I imagine they'll be coming back for you. When they do, we'll be ready."

Not one word. The priest was only trying to bait Griffin, and he wouldn't give in. He wouldn't.

"Isn't it *wonderful* how useful you are to us? First you open the way back to Earth. We might have been defeated without Earth's soldiers to add to our army. Your people have such a skill for violence—once you snip away the inconvenience of independent thought, that is."

Melanie Crowder

Griffin bared his teeth like a trapped animal. "No one would ever do a thing you said if they had a choice."

"Ah, well, *you* will."

"You're wrong!"

"Oh, no. *You* will be the one to return your parents to us. What useful trophies Philip and Katherine Fenn made. Of course, we know all about your father's skills. He'll do as we ask this time, and no world will shut us out again."

"He won't help you. No matter what you say," Griffin shot back. If there was ever a time to hide how scared he was, it was now.

"I wouldn't be so sure of that. We lacked the proper inducements before. But your father will do whatever we ask now that we have you. Such a weakness, sentimentality."

Griffin squeezed his eyes shut. He wasn't like Fi. He couldn't hide how he felt, not even to save his own life. The priest was right. His parents *would* come back for him—they were probably already scrambling to get back to Maris. And they'd do anything to keep him from suffering. Anything.

Beneath the docks, the ocean's song shifted, no longer grieving. It modulated into bright, angry notes that whipped the waves into a frenzy. Once again, the planks beneath Griffin rattled with pounding foot-steps. Uncertainty crested over the priest's face, and the soldier gripping Griffin's chin let go, whirling to face whoever approached. The priest turned too. But no one was coming for them.

Griffin craned his neck, peering between the soldier's muscled legs. The Marisians lined the docks, all facing the same direction, toward the ori-gin of the waves rolling past. Hope tore holes in the despair smothering Griffin. Maybe they could help him. Maybe they would get him out of this mess somehow.

The song rose to greet the Marisians, fierce and full. And they opened their mouths and sang back.

It wasn't like any singing Griffin had ever heard—no one on Earth had lungs like that. They poured every ounce of life into their song. Rage from years of oppression. Reverence for the power of the sea. Grief for all that was stolen from them. And love—so much greater than fear or anger or sorrow. Love, lashing like a sea serpent from their mouths.

The Marisian song met the song of the sea. The troughs of the waves fell, and the crests shot up. The priest backed away. Soldiers grabbed for their weapons, as if they could slash apart the oncoming wave, which gained height and speed until it reared twice as high as the tallest soldier. The Marisians dove from the docks, slicing through the looming wave and into the safety of the water below.

"To the boats—quick!" the priest shouted.

But it was too late. The wave crashed, sweeping everything with it—the priests and their soldiers, the guard towers, the children's toys, scattered fishing nets, and boats drying belly-up on the docks. Anything that wasn't tied down was simply gone.

The water tore at Griffin, stripping away the sweat and the terror and all remnants of the priest's threats. Griffin thrashed, trying to lift his head above water. The wave finally passed, dropping him onto the planks once again, somehow still alive. Griffin sputtered, coughing the water from his lungs and nose and sobbing in relief.

The water sluiced off him as the song of the sea calmed once again. The sun bore down overhead. Griffin's shoulders strained against the cords that lashed his wrists to the pillar. All around him, the docks groaned, split and straining against the ropes that bound them together, near collapse. Capsized boats sank beneath the water, the bubbles that rose to the surface the only sign of the priest and the soldiers sunken with them.

Thumps sounded on the planks as one by one the

people of Maris vaulted back onto the docks. Guyot and Seiche rushed to Griffin's side and pried loose the knots at his wrists and ankles.

Griffin dropped his arms, shaking them out. His hands were swollen, purple gouges in his skin where the cords had held him. It was a good thing the knots had been so tight, though, or he'd have been swept away with the rest.

"Thank you." Griffin coughed, sputtering and choking up water with his words.

"Breathe," Seiche said. "We can explain later."

Griffin felt like he'd drowned and been brought back to life. He dropped his head onto his knees, still gasping for each breath. The docks moaned, the ocean bubbling as the last guard tower toppled and sank, lost to the deep.

Guyot and Seiche knelt beside Griffin. He raised his head reluctantly, looking around at what little was left of the docks. "I've never seen anything like that," he said. "But why now? If you could sing up the waves like that, why didn't you destroy the Somnites when they first showed up?"

"Calling up the sea is not something to be taken lightly. The ocean is a raw, primal power."

"Look." Guyot pointed to the capsized boats, sinking as the waves carried them away from the docks. "Our boats have been destroyed. The docks are breaking apart. If we're lucky, we'll be able to lash together a barge of sorts. The rays and the fishes will do what they can, but we can't live like this.

"In calling up the sea to save you, we've tied our fate to yours. We won't survive without the help of our sister worlds."

Griffin accepted their offered hands, pulling himself to his feet. "I won't let you down. I promise."

GRIFFIN

WHEN GRIFFIN LANDED in the lantern room, a cry of joy escaped his lips. Somehow the impossible had actually come true. He was home. He ran his fingers along the brass fittings in the lens and wiped a trail of residue from the glass. This wasn't just any lighthouse. He'd spent nearly every day over the past three years taking care of the place with his dad. It was theirs, as much as it belonged to anyone. His parents should be here already—maybe they'd heard the alarm sound in the cottage when he came through the portal and were on their way to meet him at this very moment.

A knot formed in Griffin's throat. He turned to face the bank of windows and there it was: the cloud-covered sky, the restless gray ocean, and the impossible green of the dense forest climbing up the headland. The best of all the worlds, here, on Earth.

But *something* was different.

Griffin eased open the glass door and strode onto the gallery. The wind slapped his cheeks, carrying the smell of the little sail jellyfish that had washed up on the beach the night before. Gulls flapped and swerved in a sudden gust, squawking their indignation. Below, the water churned, pounding against the rocks. It was all so familiar, but the lighthouse felt smaller, the ocean tamer.

And then it struck him—it wasn't the lighthouse that had changed, or the rugged coast. It was him. Griffin had traveled to strange and distant worlds. He'd survived so much more than he'd ever imagined possible.

He was different.

A commotion at the base of the tower drew his attention and Griffin leaned gingerly over the railing. Coasties in crisp uniforms spilled out of the oil houses, pointing to where he stood and sprinting for the guardroom door.

"Don't move," one bellowed, adjusting a pair of bright yellow earplugs and lifting a set of bulky headphones to cover them. It was exactly as Beatrix had said—they had nothing to protect them from the priests' mind control except earplugs and some noise-canceling headphones.

Griffin reached under his tongue and dug out the pearl. Footsteps pounded up the spiral stairs. He didn't have time to take the song down to the beach like he'd planned, lay it in the sea-soaked sand, and let the lapping waves gradually make their introduction. The coast guardsmen were going to reach the lantern room any second and they wouldn't understand, not if they were expecting Somni priests coming through the portal. They definitely weren't going to give Griffin a chance to explain.

He had to trust that Beatrix was ready—that she'd found a way to spread the song inland. All he needed was to get it into the water. He balanced the pearl in his palm for a moment, then he took a step back, lunged, and hurled it over the cliff. The pearl arced through the sky, swelling and wobbling as it fell. Griffin strained, listening for the *plunk* when it hit the waves. But next thing he knew, he was thrown facedown on the steel floor, his arms pinned tight behind his back, a knee jammed into his spine.

Griffin cringed when his bruised cheek hit the ground again. He should have been scared, or worried, at least. Instead, all he felt was relief. He'd done all he could. Their fight against Somni was finally finished. Laughter shook through him as he remembered the day not so long ago when Fi had knocked him flat just like this.

"Hey—this is no laughing matter," shouted the Coastie pinning Griffin to the floor. "And this isn't a costume party. You think this is some kind of prank?"

There were a dozen of them now, crammed into the lantern room and staring menacingly at Griffin.

Why were they yelling?

The first one lifted his knee and tossed Griffin onto his back. "Oh." He paused. "I know that face." He grabbed Griffin under the arms and hefted him onto his feet. "Look! It's the kid from the photos in the cottage, the kid that went missing." He yanked the headphones off the guy closest to him. "Hey, aren't those his parents we've got at the station for questioning?"

A man with an impressive number of bars pinned to his lapel and a funny-looking hat on his head cut him off with a stern look. "What's your name, son?"

"Griffin Fenn. I'm the Assistant Lighthouse Keeper here. Or, at least, I was."

The guy in charge made a waffling motion with his hand and the guardsmen peeled off their ear protection. "You'll need to come down to the station to answer some questions, I'm afraid."

Griffin was about to begin explaining about the portal and the priests and all the rest when a sound floated in through the open gallery door, interrupting his thoughts. He started, like when you see your teacher at the hardware store in a ratty old pair of jeans—you'd recognize that face any day, but it's still the strangest thing to see it somewhere you don't expect.

The song of the sea was faint. But he would know it anywhere.

Griffin bit down on whatever it was he'd been about to say. A broad smile stretched over his face. It worked! He did it. And finally, *finally*, he was home.

GRIFFIN

T HE FENN FAMILY sat on the sofa in the sitting room of
the old cottage. A cozy fire crackled in the hearth.
They watched the waves out the picture window,
sipping their mugs of hot cocoa (with mini marsh-
mallows in one, a nip of whiskey in another, and a
dusting of cinnamon and chili powder in the third).

Suddenly the alarm blared from the cupboard
against the wall. Philip leaped up, his cocoa flying
through the air, sending chocolate drips streaming
down the freshly cleaned wallpaper.

"We really need to fix that," Katherine muttered,
shaking the cocoa off her hand. "A friendly door
chime would do."

Philip disappeared into the kitchen, reemerging
with a hand towel for each of them. "If we're going

to be having regular visitors through the portal—"

"Like Fi? How delightful. Not Arvid, certainly. Oh! How about one of those clocks with the bird that ducks in and out of those funny little doors."

"You mean a cuckoo clock?" Philip squatted beside the wall and began wiping down the wallpaper for the second time that day.

"Exactly!"

"We don't really even need an alarm anymore, do we?" Griffin hurried over to the entryway and drew his raincoat over his shoulders.

"I've got it!" Katherine leaned back into the sofa cushions, raising her cocoa to her lips again. "Glass wind chimes. Every time someone opens the portal, we get a friendly little chime to let us know. If only we knew any glassmakers who might be able to—"

"Mom. Dad!" Griffin rushed back into the sitting room, grabbed their arms, and yanked. "Come *on*. Let's go get her."

Katherine hauled herself off the sofa with a chuckle. "I'm dying to see Fi too."

Griffin bounded out the door and down the cottage stairs. "She's never even seen the ocean!"

The council between worlds met on the lighthouse lawn at midnight. The ocean is a stunner all the time, but at night, when you can't see the thing that roars at you, it's even more magnificent.

Only this ocean didn't just roar. It sang.

The song had shifted in the days since it was first introduced to Earth. After all, it had different creatures to woo, and the strange sensation of rocks and sands beating at its edges. The song rose with each crashing wave, keening like humpbacks in the deep, and it fell back in each lapse between sets, gurgling and whispering, coaxing the critters on the beach to join in.

Griffin ran the last few steps, only to stop short of where Fi stood with Liv and her aunt Ada, suddenly overcome with shyness. Guyot and Seiche were there from Maris. Arvid had come from Somni, and Leónie from Caligo. Of course, Beatrix was there with the assembled Keepers. Griffin was about to cross the space between them to say hi to Fi when Beatrix stepped up to speak.

"Welcome, everyone. This is a day most of us never thought would come. A joyous day. But our work is not finished yet."

"Indeed," Arvid said. "We've come to ask the help of the greenwitches in bringing the sjel trees to the surface of Somni again. We have so few seeds stored—we worry we're already past the tipping point."

Liv countered, "And we would collect Vinea's dead from Somni and lay them to rest in the green."

Seiche stepped in. "We ask help rebuilding our boats."

"And we can't forget," Katherine added, "Arida and Glacies are still waiting to be freed."

"Well, someone should tell Stella the priests are gone. They may want nothing to do with us, but we should invite them to join the council, all the same."

Beatrix held up a hand. "Yes. We will reach out to the lost worlds."

The circle buzzed with noise as the adults dithered and demurred, not exactly arguing, but definitely not in agreement over how, exactly, they were going to accomplish all that. Griffin rolled his eyes. He'd seen this before, on every single world he'd visited. Only this time, he didn't care what the adults decided. He had his parents back, Fi was safe, and the council wouldn't stop until the priests had been defeated, on every world.

Things would never be the same again. Magic from Maris had saved Earth. Magic from Caligo had saved Vinea's raze crews. And magic from Vinea would bring back Somni's sjel trees. Who knew what Glacies might offer the council, or Arida, or Stella?

Griffin caught Fi's eye and jerked his head to the side. He backed away from the circle, and toward the cliff's edge. Fi ran up and threw her arms around him. "I heard what you did on Maris." She pulled back just far enough that she could punch him playfully in the arm.

Griffin blushed. "Just trying to keep up with you—I mean, look at you. You *glow*. With, um, magic."

She snorted. "Yeah, I guess I do. You *have* to come to Vinea and see the wildlands for yourself. It'll take years to really come back, but it's already started healing."

Griffin laughed. "I get it, I get it, Vinea's pretty great. But I bet they don't have hot cocoa."

They trotted down the path leading to the little cottage, but rather than racing between the trees as Griffin liked to do, Fi paused to inspect every single leaf and moss and vine along the way. Finally, his excitement to have her here erased the last of his shyness and Griffin grabbed Fi's hand, tugging her along with him. Together they ran along the winding path, their laughter ringing through the forest and startling the birds from the trees. The highest branches stretched toward the girl with the green magic in her veins, while the song of the sea sang for the boy who'd carried it to this wondrous new world. And above it all, the lighthouse beams shone, winking as they whirled out of sight.

MANY THANKS TO

Reka Simonsen

Justin Chanda

Julia McCarthy

Jeannie Ng

Alison Velea

Debra Sfetsios-Conover

Kailey Whitman

Ammi-Joan Paquette

Lauren Sabel

Emily France

Meg Wiviott

Jennifer Bertman

Cammen Lowstuter

Whitney Walker